Pat Rylance,

"Ty Cynwyd",

Llangynwyd,

Nr. Bridgend.

Glam.

"WHAT'S WRONG, MY DEAR?" ASKED DELIA GENTLY

(From " Perpetual Calm ")

# IDEAL BOOK

## *for*

# GIRLS

### DEAN & SON, LTD.

41/43 LUDGATE HILL, LONDON, E.C.4

Sole Agents for South Africa: Central News Agency, Ltd.
Sole Agents for Australia and New Zealand: Gordon and Gotch, Ltd.

*Made and Printed in Great Britain*

# CONTENTS

# PERPETUAL CALM

by WINIFRED NORLING

D ELIA ARMSTRONG lay in the hammock, swinging gently to and fro, an unopened book and a box of chocolates beside her. She was a pretty girl, with deep blue eyes and golden-brown hair that curled attractively round her expressive face. Usually she was smiling, but today she looked seriously into space, her forehead slightly puckered in thought. She seemed to be watching for something, and a few minutes later the sound of an approaching car broke the stillness of the summer afternoon. It came to a stop before the front door of Golden Acres, and people alighted, but still Delia did not move. There was now a sad look in her eyes, and her lips were set in a mutinous line.

It was not long before a tall dark figure emerged from the house and slowly crossed the lawn towards the now motionless hammock. In his hand he carried a small silver salver, on which lay a visiting card.

"Mr. and Miss Dunthorpe have arrived, Miss Delia, and wish to see you. I have put them in the drawing-room."

"Thank you, Graham. I will come in. Is—is he nice?" she went on in a rather different voice, for she and the butler were old friends. "I dread the thought of a guardian, Graham, after dear Aunt Ermentrude."

"That is only natural, Miss Delia, for her ladyship was one in a thousand. I'd never stay on at Golden Acres now she's gone, if it weren't for you. Mr. Dunthorpe's a pleasant-spoken gentleman if a bit brusque. He seems in a hurry, miss, if you'll forgive my mentioning it."

Gracefully Delia swung herself to the ground.

"And the daughter?" she asked the hovering butler.

"As pretty as a picture and most pleasant," Graham replied, his usually mask-like face relaxing. "She's about your age, Miss Delia, and her father called her Jasmine."

"Thanks, Graham. I'll go to meet my fate. It's useless skulking here repining. Wish me luck."

The old butler stood watching the graceful figure moving towards the fine old Jacobean manor. There was an anxious look in his faded blue eyes.

"Poor Miss Delia!" he murmured. "She'll miss the mistress more and more, I'm afraid. This guardian of hers isn't like her ladyship; kind maybe, but he won't indulge the little mistress as her aunt did. And from what Mr. Raymond let drop when he came to read the will, I'm afraid we're in for changes. Not that I need worry, thanks to her ladyship, but 'twill break Miss Delia's heart if she has to leave Golden Acres."

Never for a moment dreaming of such a possibility, Delia crossed the hall. At the drawing-room door she paused for an instant in an attempt to repress the unusual feeling of apprehension that flooded her. She was not shy, and she usually enjoyed meeting people. Why did she not want to meet her guardian and his daughter? As she stood there, a voice cut across her thoughts.

"Of course she must know, Jasmine. Don't be foolish. I don't believe in beating about the bush. You always say you like my directness."

"I do, Dads, but I'm different. I know and understand you. Delia's not used to men. From what Mr. Raymond says, she's been indulged and

# PERPETUAL CALM

coddled and reared like a fairy-tale princess. You'll have to handle her with velvet gloves. She——"

Delia flung open the door, her face flaming. She gave Jasmine a look that told that young lady she had been overheard, then walked straight up to her guardian and held out her hand.

"How do you do, Mr. Dunthorpe? Welcome to Golden Acres. I hope Graham offered you refreshment. He's a good butler, but he is no longer young, and my aunt's death has upset him. He could retire, of course, but he wishes to stay on with me, and I shall naturally keep him. I prefer his loyalty and faithful service to greater efficiency."

For a moment Basil Dunthorpe did not speak. He regarded Delia thoughtfully; then he said:

"How old are you, Delia?"

"Sixteen. Nearly grown up, in fact. Had Aunt Ermentrude lived, I suppose I should have stayed at school till I was eighteen, but now I must leave and attend to things here. I have already written to Miss Hillditch of Clodean College and explained matters."

"Indeed! You appear to have taken everything for granted and left little to your new guardian," said Basil Dunthorpe drily. "I'm afraid you are in for a series of shocks, Delia. First and foremost, you will have to leave Golden Acres."

"Leave Golden Acres!" repeated Delia in dazed tones. "I can't believe you realise what you are saying, Mr. Dunthorpe."

"Indeed I do, only too well. And hadn't you better call me Cousin Basil? We are related, you know, and you and Jasmine are sort of cousins."

"Yes, Delia, we are, and we needn't remember the times removed, need we? I shall love having a sister. It's not much fun being an only child, is it?"

"I've never had a family, and I don't want one now," snapped Delia. "Why must I leave Golden Acres, Mr. Dunthorpe?" she went on, ignoring Jasmine.

"Lack of money," returned her guardian briefly. "Golden Acres must be let to help pay the many annuities and bequests in your aunt's will. You will come to live with us. There will be enough money to pay for you to go to the local High School with Jasmine, and to feed and clothe you. You won't be dependent on us, but you can only manage if you share our home. Jasmine is very eager to have you, and I hope you will be happy in Hampstead."

"Hampstead!" The contempt in Delia's voice brought the colour to Jasmine's usually pale cheeks. "Isn't that a suburb of London? I can hardly imagine myself settling in suburbia. Aunt Ermentrude and I often laughed at such places and the people who lived there with their lace curtains and aspidistras."

"You have much to learn, Delia, and I'm afraid you won't find it easy. Your aunt has done you more harm than you know, and——"

"How dare you sneer at my aunt and criticise her treatment of me?" stormed Delia. "She was good and kind, and everybody loved her. The world is a poorer place without her, and I—I hate you and Jasmine."

The heavy silence that filled the room made Delia realise what she had done.

"Forgive me," she apologised. "I ought not to have spoken to you like that, but I was fond of my aunt and can't bear to hear her criticised. She has been everything to me, and I miss her more than words can say. I'm sure you mean to be kind, Cousin Basil, but I couldn't be happy in a suburb of London. If there is not enough money for me to stay on at Golden Acres, I could live in one of the estate houses with Marjorie— my old nurse—and her young niece Betty. You need not worry about me. Surely there is sufficient money for that, since I should not need school fees, and little for clothes and upkeep."

"I daresay it could be managed financially, but I—as your guardian —cannot allow it. Your education is not finished, and you are far too young to be buried alive with no one of your own age or class. You will come to us as I have arranged, and I hope you will fit in and accommodate yourself to your changed circumstances."

"Don't look like that, Delia," cried Jasmine. "It's quite a nice house, really, and the High School's super. We'll give you a good time there, and you'll soon love it."

"Hardly, after Clodean College," said Delia with a slight sneer. "I shan't go to school. If you force me to live with you till I am twenty-one I suppose I must, Cousin Basil, but I will *not* go to a cheap day school."

For a moment Basil Dunthorpe looked as though he intended to say a great deal; but, instead, he just cleared his throat and looked at the angry girl before him. When he spoke, his voice was very kind.

"I'm sorry, my dear, to be the bearer of bad news. You will feel leaving this beautiful place, but I can assure you it is necessary if people like your old butler are to get their annuities. Your aunt was too generous, Delia, and she would not be advised by Frank Raymond. We shall welcome you to our home, Jasmine and I, and we shall try to make you happy. Won't you meet us half-way?"

Tears sprang to Delia's eyes, but she proudly blinked them back.

"If I must come to you, I must," she declared. "I would rather be sacrificed than allow people like Graham to suffer. When must I leave here?"

"Before the end of the month. If you arrive early in September, you will have time to settle in before the new term begins on the fifteenth. If there is anything I can do to help you, let me know."

"I suppose I may bring my personal belongings with me?" asked Delia in expressionless tones.

"Of course. We will try to make the change as easy as possible for you. You have always had everything you could possibly want, I know, but remember, my dear, perpetual calm never made a sailor."

Delia was to remember those words during the next weeks. As one link after another with her old life was severed, she realised how true they were. She had never had to do anything for herself while her aunt was alive, hardly to think, but now she began to realise she had feet and must learn to stand on them. The waves of circumstance were teaching her to swim not only *with* but *against* the current, and although she did not know it yet, she was to find adversity's hidden jewel in a way she little guessed.

Basil Dunthorpe came frequently to Golden Acres, but he did not again bring Jasmine. He discussed many things with Delia, but school was never mentioned, to Delia's secret relief, for she was determined not to go to the High School with Jasmine.

At last the day came when Delia had to say goodbye to Golden Acres. Her guardian had come for her in his car, and the journey to London was a quiet one. The look of suffering in Delia's face kept Basil Dunthorpe silent after a few awkward attempts at conversation.

They reached Hampstead in time for tea, and Jasmine greeted Delia warmly.

"I'm so glad you've come, Delia," she declared. "Your room is quite ready. All your things are up there, and we hope you will like the way we've arranged them. If not, they can be changed. I expect you'd like a wash before tea, wouldn't you?"

"Yes, please. I feel horribly dusty and tired. Do you think I could have a cup of tea in my room? I really don't feel like coming down and talking."

"Of course," Jasmine answered quickly. "I'll bring it up myself. Is there anything you'd particularly like?"

"No thanks. I'm not hungry. You needn't bother to be polite, Jasmine. I know you must hate my being here as much as I loathe coming."

"But I don't," objected Jasmine. "Honestly I don't. I want you, Delia. I realise how you must feel leaving Golden Acres for this, but I've always wanted a sister, and I think you're tops."

Delia smiled.

"That's sweet of you, my dear, and if we hadn't been forced together so remorselessly, we might have been friends. But I can't accept your overtures, feeling as I do about your father."

"Oh, I know Daddy *sounds* a bear, but his growl is worse than his bite," said Jasmine easily. "When you get to know him, you'll just *have* to like him. He hated uprooting you, I know, but he felt it had to be. I hope you won't be awfully dull here. It'll be better when school begins."

"When's that? Next Thursday week, isn't it?"

"Yes. The old High's a decent hole, even if it's not Clodean College. Most of the girls will welcome you, and Miss Rankin's a sporty type for a headmistress."

"Is she?" Delia's tone was so snubbing that Jasmine fled in search of tea.

In the days that followed there were no outward signs of animosity, but Jasmine felt all was not well. Almost every day Delia went off on her own, not refusing but merely ignoring the younger girl's advances. Jasmine longed to know what her cousin was doing, but was too proud and shy to ask. Mr. Dunthorpe said little, hoping that the girls were making friends and that Delia would be amenable and cause no trouble.

It was two days before school began that Delia quietly exploded her bombshell, at breakfast time, soon after she had read her letters. One she kept in her hand, and there was an excited gleam in her eyes as she quietly said:

"I shan't be able to go to school after all, Cousin Basil. You see, I've taken a job."

Basil Dunthorpe dropped his paper and looked at Delia over the top of his spectacles.

"You've what?" he demanded.

"Taken a job. Quite a respectable one with a decent salary."

"Indeed! Where?"

"At Henriette's, the hat shop. Madame is very pleasant, and we like each other. I've been to see her twice, and I have thought the whole matter over most carefully. I'm too old to begin at a fresh school, and if money's so short, it's only fair that I should earn some."

"It's not as short as all that," snorted Mr. Dunthorpe irritably. "I told you that there was sufficient to pay your school fees and keep you here. Jasmine was very ready to share, and——"

"I know," cut in Delia, "but I'd hate to deprive her. I shall be really independent now. I hope you won't have to pay half a term's fees, Cousin Basil. I couldn't tell you sooner, because I did not know myself till this letter from Madame arrived."

"Is it that jolly shop in the Grove, Delia?" asked Jasmine eagerly. "What will you have to do?"

"Be in the shop when wanted to show off hats to the more important customers, and help behind the scenes with ideas and designing. Madame seems to think I have a flair for colour. I didn't know I had, but I do know what I like and why. Aunt Ermentrude had excellent taste, and I suppose I've learned a lot without realising it. The first time I went to see Madame I made a few useful suggestions, and I think I shall quite enjoy the life. There's money in it, and as I have to make what I want now, I may as well begin at once. I take it you have no objections, Cousin Basil?"

"Rather late in the day to ask me that," snapped Mr. Dunthorpe. "Of course I don't approve, and I still feel you ought to go to school.

Your education isn't finished, and you'll regret it later if I give way to you now. You'll grow up an ignoramus, and be at a disadvantage all through life."

"Brains aren't everything," argued Delia. "In fact, men hate women to be bluestockings, and money opens most doors. I shall succeed. In any case, let me try for a few months. If by Christmas I've not proved a success, I'll go to school in January. Is that a bargain?"

"Oh yes, Daddy, do let her try," begged Jasmine. "Frankly, I wish I'd thought of it. I love school, of course, but being in a shop would be great fun, and hats can be so ridiculously fascinating these days."

"Thought you never wore one except for church," said Basil Dunthorpe, regarding his daughter in surprise.

"I don't, but I shall when I'm older, and I shall be glad to have Delia choose them for me at cheap rates."

Suddenly Basil Dunthorpe laughed.

"What can a mere male do against you?" he questioned. "And I haven't even Frank Raymond to support me. I will go and see this Madame somebody, Delia, and let you know my decision later. When had you planned to begin work?"

"Next Monday. I didn't see any point in waiting. I have a black afternoon frock that will do for the salon, and fortunately I'm not shy and can talk to strangers easily."

And so the next week Delia Armstrong, the pampered niece of the wealthy Lady Ermentrude Villiers, went to Henriette's at a commencing salary of two pounds five shillings a week. On the Monday morning Jasmine accompanied her cousin as far as the shop, and the two girls were nearer to each other than they had been since their meeting.

"I almost envy you," sighed Jasmine. "You look so smart and sophisticated in black, and I feel such a gawky schoolgirl. Wish I could trim hats and were coming with you."

Delia regarded her cousin thoughtfully. Then she shook her head.

"It wouldn't suit you, Jasmine. You're far happier hitting a ball about in a muddy field than you would be modelling hats. Here we are. Good-bye for now."

"Goodbye and good luck. Shall I call for you tonight about six? I can easily, if you'd like me to, but I don't want to be a nuisance."

"I'll be glad to have you," Delia assured her cordially, as she dis-appeared through the side door of the smart gold and cream shop.

Henrietta Brant greeted her kindly and showed her where to put her things. The milliner owed much of her success to personal attention. She was always there—the first to arrive, the last to leave. Her staff knew this, and they respected Madame's keenness and rarely slacked themselves.

When she liked, Delia could be very charming, and she soon became popular with the rest of the staff. True, at first they rather resented the way in which Madame favoured her, but common sense won. It was easy to see that Delia had an unusual gift for designing. She always knew just which feather to use, and how to fix a bow or a spray of flowers. It was this gift which brought her more and more into the workroom, where she met Maisie Dobson. Although only a year younger than Delia, Maisie seemed quite a child, young and inexperienced, and at everyone's beck and call. It was "Do this, Maisie" or "Fetch that, Maisie" from morning till night, just as though she were a machine. Usually she was even-tempered and sunny, and so Delia was more than a little surprised to find her one evening in floods of tears. Delia had stayed late to finish a hat, and Maisie had been kept to deliver it when it was ready.

"Here's the hat, Maisie," cried Delia, hurrying into the workroom. "Sorry I couldn't finish it sooner."

Maisie did not answer. She just sat there, sobbing.

"What's wrong, my dear?" asked Delia gently, putting down the gaily striped hat box and slipping an arm round the pathetic little figure. "Have you had bad news? Can't you tell me? Sometimes a trouble shared is a trouble halved."

"It's—it's Mother," sobbed Maisie. "I promised to visit her tonight, and now I'll be too late."

"Surely not, Maisie. It's not far to Frensham Avenue, and you'll still have lots of the evening left. Where is your mother?"

"In hospital, Miss Delia, and the visiting hours are over at seven. I wanted to take her some flowers, too. I've been saving up, and now I've lost my purse."

"We'll find it, Maisie; don't cry. I'll lend you ten bob, and we'll find your purse tomorrow. It's only twenty-past six, so you'll be in time if you cut off to the hospital straight away. I'll deliver the hat."

"Oh, Miss Delia! But what will Madame say?"

"Nothing. I'll square her. I can't think why you didn't tell her about your mother. She wouldn't have kept you if she'd known. She's terribly kind."

"Is she? She's so strict, and she frightens me. I was afraid she'd sack me if I questioned waiting, and we need the money more than ever with Mother ill. Ann is still at school, you see, and then there are the twins. Father only has part-time work, and Mother helps out with dressmaking. I helped her when I first left school, but we needed more money, and Madame knew Mother years ago and offered to take me. I'm not clever like Ann, and I couldn't win a scholarship."

"I see. Well, take this note and cut along. Take the flowers from us both, then you needn't pay back the money. I'm not short. Hurry."

Maisie hurried, and the next day she greeted Delia shyly, but with a look of devotion in her eyes that embarrassed the elder girl.

"Mother's better, Miss Delia, and she loved the flowers. I only spent two shillings on them, but could I give you the change when I get my money? I—I'm afraid I used some of it at the grocer's, and they wouldn't let me have Jackie's boots unless I paid for the repairs, and his others let in water."

"Keep it, Maisie," said Delia easily. "I'm not short, and your purse will turn up. I'm glad your mother is better. How long will she still be in hospital?"

"Several weeks, I'm afraid. She worries a lot about us, and Nurse says that keeps her back. Ann's going to see her today, and I shall go with Father on Sunday."

"Do you think she'd like me to go one day, Maisie?" asked Delia. "I could tell her all about you and the work here."

"Oh, Miss Delia, would you?" Maisie's eyes were shining. "She'd love it. When could you go?"

"Any time, almost. Would Friday evening fit?"

"Rather! I'll tell Dad, and he'll be ever so pleased."

"Can your mother eat fruit, or would she rather have soap or sweets?"

"She'd like anything," declared Maisie. "We can't take her much, and they do compare so in the ward. Not Mother, but the rest."

Delia went on the Friday evening to see Mrs. Dobson. She did not tell them at home where she was going, because she was afraid Mr. Dunthorpe might make a fuss. She found Mrs. Dobson a pleasant well-spoken woman who was devoted to her family and eager to hear anything about Maisie.

"It's a chance for her, and I do hope she gets on. She's not like Ann, who loves books, but she has a good eye for colour and is original. I should have liked to apprentice her properly, but we hadn't the money. I think she could design and I hope Madame will try her out later.

"I do a lot of the designing, and I'll give her a try-out some time," Delia promised.

After that, Delia was always sending Mrs. Dobson presents and giving things to Maisie for the children. Although Maisie's purse was found— one of the girls had picked it up and put it in her bag by mistake— Delia refused to take back any of the ten shillings. A strange friendship sprang up between the two girls, and Maisie told Delia all about the Dobsons' troubles. When Ann needed a new hockey stick, Delia wormed the information out of Maisie and bought one. When Jackie outgrew his coat, it was Delia who got him a new one. She bought little Jill a winter dress, and on her birthday made Maisie everlastingly happy by giving her a wristlet watch.

Jasmine noticed a subtle change in her cousin, and it puzzled her. She seemed perpetually short of cash, and once she even borrowed five shillings from Jasmine. She repaid it promptly, but Jasmine was worried. On what was Delia spending her money? Forty-five shillings every week seemed untold wealth to Jasmine, whose weekly pocket money was only half a crown. Could Delia be in trouble? Had she got herself into a mess by buying too many expensive luxuries? Jasmine rarely met her cousin in the evenings now, for she seemed to always have an engagement after working hours, and Jasmine could not bring herself to spy on Delia.

"Like me to meet you tonight, Delia?" she asked one day.

"No thanks, Jasmine. I'm going out with one of the girls."

"Lucky you. You're always off somewhere jolly and exciting, while I have to stodge away at my prep."

Delia did not answer, but she smiled rather wryly. Visiting a sick woman in hospital and trying to do good by stealth brought their own reward, but they were neither jolly nor exciting.

"Can you lend me ten bob, Delia?" asked Jasmine another day. "I've some subs that must be paid, and Daddy's away till Saturday, as you know."

"I can let you have it on Friday, but I'm broke till then. Will that do?" Delia questioned. "I'm sorry I haven't it now."

"So am I. You do spend a lot, Delia. If I had your screw, I'd be rolling."

"Perhaps, but I'm not," said Delia shortly. "You can have it on Friday. Why not ask Nandy, as you call her? She has the housekeeping money and will give *you* anything. Wish I had *my* old nurse here. She adored me, and I loved her next best to Aunt Ermentrude."

"I think I will. I *must* have it tomorrow," Jasmine explained, before hurrying off.

One day Delia met Ann Dobson and heard more about the High School than she had ever done from Jasmine. To Ann it was the be-all and end-all. She adored Miss Hewitt, and lived for the chance to do something outstanding for the school that had opened its doors to a mere scholarship girl.

"I expect you know my cousin Jasmine Dunthorpe," said Delia, for the want of something better to say.

"Is Jasmine your cousin?  She's marvellous!  She plays for the First Hockey Eleven and is absolutely wizard at gym.  She'll be a prefect next year.  She's tremendously popular.  I like her awfully."

"I'm surprised she hasn't asked you home to tea if you're chums. She often brings in school friends."

"Oh, we're not friends.  Why, I'm only a scholarship kid."

"And I'm only a shop girl," laughed Delia.  "Jasmine's not a snob. What about you and Maisie both coming to tea next Saturday?  Your father would look after Jackie and Jill, wouldn't he?"

"We—we'd like to if you're sure your people won't mind, Miss Delia," declared Maisie.

"Good, but for heaven's sake call me Delia out of business hours. It may be necessary to make distinctions at Henriette's, but it isn't otherwise.  You're going to be a famous designer one day, Maisie, or my name's not Delia Armstrong.  We're planning to open an exclusive establishment in Mayfair, Ann, and Maisie's going to be a sort of hat Hartnell to the Queen.  We'll have special black and gold hat boxes for delivery to Buckingham Palace."

They all laughed, but Maisie's eyes were shining.

"I'm glad you think I may be some good one day," she said.  "Madame saw that green and tan beret I was working out, and she liked it.  I'm to do other drawings and show her."

"I know.  She told me.  If I'm not careful, you'll be pinching my laurels," Delia laughed.  "Still, London's a big place, and there'll be room for both of us.  We'll be in partnership, and so I needn't worry."

If Jasmine was surprised to hear that Ann Dobson was coming to tea, she did not show it.  Although she had had little to do with her, she liked the scholarship girl.

"I didn't know you knew my cousin Delia," she said to her.

"Yes. She and Maisie both work at Henriette's, and Delia's been simply super to us. She's sent Mother wonderful presents all the time she's been in hospital, and she bought me a new hockey stick, and gave Maisie a longed-for watch on her birthday. She spoils the twins, too. She must have lots of money. I've often wondered why she works for Madame."

"She only has her salary," Jasmine told her, "though that's all hers. She hasn't to pay for her keep like most working girls. All the same, she must find it difficult to manage after having everything she wanted at Golden Acres. I'm beginning to think Delia has what it takes, and I take off my hat to her."

"Maisie adores her, and with good reason. All of us Dobsons owe her more than we can ever repay."

Christmas came, and Delia had proved her worth. There was no talk of her returning to school. She and Maisie now designed many of Henriette's most popular hats, and they were both earning more money.

"Glad I uprooted you, Delia?" Basil Dunthorpe asked one day. "You seem to have found your feet."

"I have. I'm a sailor now, and I shouldn't have been if I'd gone on existing in a state of perpetual calm. I hated coming here, but I love my life now and wouldn't even exchange it for Golden Acres. It's wonderful to have a career, and when we open our Mayfair shop with Delise over the door, you, Cousin Basil, and Jasmine will—I hope—be among our guests at our first hat show. If only Aunt Ermentrude could have been there, too! But you're proud of me now, aren't you?"

"Yes, my dear, I am. We've grown to understand and respect each other. I'm glad that I was made your guardian and that I dragged you to Hampstead."

"So am I," Delia agreed. "Thank you, Guardy darling."

# ILONKA GOES TO LIVERPOOL

### By MABEL E. ALLAN

"OH, shall we never get to Liverpool?" sighed Ilonka Barrington, pressing her nose close to the carriage window, through which she could see nothing but darkness. The express was going along fairly steadily now, but ever since they had left Rugby there had been delays.

"There must be fog all along the line," remarked the woman opposite, waking up from her restless sleep for a moment.

Ilonka sighed gustily and then, taking up her magazine again, settled down in her corner and tried to read. But she could not keep her eyes on the printed words for more than a minute at a time. The train had left Euston at a quarter to four and by now it should have been in Liverpool. Oh, how wretched and horrible it was coming to Liverpool alone in the Christmas holidays!

Liverpool! How miserable it sounded. Ilonka had never been there, but she imagined it as grey and dismal and depressing, dim with factory smoke and sea fog. Grim grey houses and people with dreadful nasal voices! Did anyone interesting ever live in Liverpool?

She was going to spend three weeks there with Aunt Clare—absolutely unknown Aunt Clare! And with Lizzie, too. It was the prospect of meeting Lizzie, also completely unknown, that had made Ilonka feel worse, somehow.

She looked back over the past three days miserably. Holidays had always been such fun in the rather haphazard little flat in London. When Daddy was not writing they usually went out a great deal, to exhibitions, films, and new and interesting plays, and *how* she had been looking forward to it this time after a particularly dull school term! And then Daddy had suddenly been asked to write a special article. He had said:

"Ilonka, you can't stop here alone while I am working, and most of our friends have gone away for Christmas or are overcrowded already. Write to Aunt Clare. I believe she lives in Liverpool. Her address is on a piece of paper in the *Oxford Dictionary*."

How like Daddy that had been! Aunt Clare was their only relation and Ilonka had scarcely ever heard anything about her. She had searched for the address, feeling depressed and disappointed.

She found Aunt Clare's address, which her father had written in his sprawling writing. "Mrs. Lenning, Mockbeggar, East Road, Egremont," and wrote off at once, adding Liverpool to the address, since she had always heard that Aunt Clare lived there.

Aunt Clare sent a letter by return,

"Come at once, dear Ilonka," wrote Aunt Clare, "I shall be so pleased to have you. I have often thought we should meet. You will be company for me and Lizzie. Lizzie is lonely at times, I am sure, though she says not. She is away at the moment, but——"

"Bother, bother Lizzie!" Ilonka thought, crumpling the letter. "I expect she's fifty and awfully dull, and Aunt Clare sounds a vague old thing. I suppose she's a little like Daddy. *He's* certainly vague. So someone will meet me at Liverpool! How beastly it all is!"

She had sat for all these hours in the train feeling increasingly sorry for herself. The fact that the express had lost time and was very late had made things worse.

"I just wish Lizzie would stop floating about in my mind!" grumbled Ilonka to herself, staring fixedly at her magazine. "I'd sooner have Aunt Clare alone; the last thing I want is to be company for Lizzie! Who is she, anyway? Some sort of companion or lodger, I suppose. Did anyone ever hear of anything so dismal as Christmas in Liverpool with someone who is lonely, called Lizzie!"

After what seemed a very long time, and after crossing many points, the train drew up in a huge, dim station, where fog wreathed round the lamps. Could this be Liverpool? She sprang up in a panic, then sank down again as a porter rushed past, yelling: "Crewe! Crewe! Liverpool train!"

Crewe! Well, that was nearly as bad as Liverpool! But could Liverpool be any worse? Ilonka was peering out fretfully, her smooth black hair falling forward over her cheeks, when someone passed along the corridor, paused, then turned back and pushed open the door of the compartment.

From her father Ilonka had learned at a very early age to appreciate beauty; beauty in words, in pictures, in personality, in people's faces. The sight of the girl who was entering made her feel better at once. She was about eighteen, with soft chestnut hair, a perfectly shaped, rather pale face, and eyes that were a wonderful clear grey. The most noticeable thing about her, however, was that she looked as though she could be gay, really gay and jolly.

"Well, if she's going to Liverpool, too, I don't mind so much!" Ilonka found herself thinking illogically. For what could it matter where the girl was going?

Ilonka sighed and flicked the pages of her magazine. The girl turned to her with a little smile.

"The train's very late, isn't it? I'm nearly frozen to death with walking up and down in this fog, but the waiting-room was so dismal. Was it foggy in London? Have you come from there?"

"Yes, I have," said Ilonka, "and it wasn't foggy at all. I suppose it will be in Liverpool?"

"Quite likely," said the stranger, but did not sound as though she minded very much.

"Do you know Liverpool well?" Ilonka found herself asking. "Do tell me about it. I hate the thought of going there. I've been hating the place all the way up. Is it very awful?"

The stranger laughed.

"Oh, well, I don't know. It's full of character, at any rate. I shouldn't hate it till you get there and see for yourself. Whereabouts are you going?"

And then Ilonka found herself telling the whole story; all about Daddy and Aunt Clare's address, and about the letter and Lizzie—how she hated the thought of Lizzie! Then she flushed and said:

"I'm sorry. I'd better snap out of it. Daddy always hates people to be sorry for themselves."

"Still, I expect it's done you good to talk about it," said the stranger, seeming to understand how lonely the last three days had been.

Meanwhile, the train had progressed on its way to Liverpool, but certainly not in the manner expected of an express.

"We're going to be hours late," said the stranger. "Is someone meeting you?"

"Yes, Aunt Clare, I suppose. How shall we get to this place? By bus?" She waved the address under the girl's nose.

"By boat," said she, calmly.

"Boat? Why by boat?"

"Well, because it isn't Liverpool at all that you're going to. At least, you *are* going there, but then you leave it again. Egremont is just across the river—the Mersey, you know. You cross by ferryboat, and so do I, for I live over there. It's grand in a fog; I always love it."

The stranger talked easily and cheerfully in low tones, while everyone else dozed and slept. It appeared she was a student at Liverpool Art

School. She talked of her friends and of the different branches of art that they were studying, and Ilonka talked eagerly, too, for it was a subject very near her heart. Her name, it appeared, was Magnolia Dennis.

"Awful, isn't it?" she said. "People always groan."

"Mine's nearly as bad," said Ilonka. "Mother was Hungarian—that explains it. Please tell me more about the things you do."

She had never imagined talking so easily to a stranger, but the journey was so long-drawn-out and she had been so lonely and unhappy, that she was doubly glad of the companionship. At the back of her mind she hoped to see Magnolia Dennis again.

At last, after what seemed an endless succession of tunnels, the train slid into Lime Street Station, Liverpool, nearly three hours late. Thick fog dimmed the lights and it was very cold. Ilonka stayed close to her new friend as they were jostled towards the barrier. She felt very much alone arriving in this northern seaport so late, and she began to hope that Aunt Clare *was* there to meet her. But though she looked about hopefully, no one came up to her. She waited till nearly everyone had gone, then turned to Magnolia still standing nearby.

"What shall I do? It was nice of you to wait. How do I get to the ferry?"

"There's no hope of a taxi, I'm afraid," said Magnolia. "Not unless we wait. We'd better go by tram."

"Lucky I sent on most of my luggage this morning," said Ilonka, as they left the station side by side. "Oh, I am glad I met you!"

A rattling tramcar took them down to the pier head and the sound of the fog-horns sent a little thrill up Ilonka's spine. It sounded like the dear, familiar Thames, and it was exciting to be crossing a strange river in fog at nearly eleven at night.

"Can we go on deck?" she asked, and Magnolia laughed.

"Yes, we can. But aren't you too cold? Hadn't we better be stuffy and sit inside?"

"Well, it *is* cold, but I like the feeling of being on the river in the fog.

An adventurous sort of feeling. Listen to the bell on the other side. What's over there? I wish my geography was better!"

"It's Cheshire over there. I'm glad you like it," said Magnolia, as they stood in the bow peering through the fog. "You feel more cheerful, don't you? Do you still loathe coming to Liverpool?"

"No-o-o, not so much. You made me feel better talking about the art school and theatres. It's only—oh, bother Lizzie! I'm sure she's simply awful. I don't want to be company for her."

"I should wait until you see her," said Magnolia sensibly.

"I don't need to. I'm dreading it! I say, can I—would you—is there any hope that I might see you again?"

Magnolia hesitated and when she spoke her voice was a little odd.

"Well, yes. I should think there is."

Instantly Ilonka thought:

"Of course, she doesn't want me! I'm only sixteen and she must have heaps of friends. What an ass I was to risk a snub!"

She was very silent during the rest of the crossing. Magnolia hurried her off the boat.

"Hurry, then we may snatch a taxi. I daresay the last bus has gone."

They did "snatch" a taxi, and Ilonka climbed in thankfully, though still feeling sore and resentful. She asked:

"Where are you going? Which of us is to be dropped first?"

"Oh, you," said Magnolia, and the taxi drove off through the mist.

After about ten minutes of slow travelling it drew up and Ilonka heard the sound of the river breaking against a seawall.

"Why! Are we still near the water?"

"Yes, your aunt's house is really on the Promenade. It only just happens that the front gate is in East Road." Magnolia paid the driver and took Ilonka by the arm.

"But—but—your taxi!" For the man had shut the door and the vehicle was fast disappearing.

"I don't want it," said Magnolia, leading her new friend under a stone archway and up a stone-flagged path, dimly lighted by a lamp. A door was flung open and a voice called, "Is that you, Lizzie? Did you find her? Oh, what a night! I've been so worried!"

"It was all right. I found her on the train. And we got a taxi," said Magnolia cheerfully.

Ilonka stood in the doorway staring from her aunt to the girl she had grown to like so much in so short a time.

"Lizzie! But—I don't understand."

"It was a mean trick to play. Oh, come in and have a hot drink. It's all right, Mrs. Lenning. We haven't both gone silly. This is your niece, Ilonka Barrington."

Over a huge supper, Magnolia explained.

"You see, I live here. I haven't any parents or relations and Mrs. Lenning has sort of adopted me. She won't call me Magnolia. She likes good plain names." She smiled very affectionately at the elderly lady. "So she calls me Lizzie. I've been visiting friends who live outside Crewe and she rang me up this morning and explained about you. I was going to meet you at the barrier at Lime Street, but I suddenly thought that if I was lucky I might see you on the train. I *thought* it must be you, because I could see I.B. on a case in the rack above your head. And I just couldn't resist keeping quiet about who I was. You *were* miserable, weren't you? Do you still hate Lizzie?"

Ilonka blushed scarlet. "I was a little ass! Oh, will you be friends, please, Magnolia Dennis? And *may* I come to the party at the art school?"

"Of course, to both. And I was dying to tell you about the house when you were moaning about Liverpool. It's most terribly old and there are heaps of smuggling stories, and even a secret passage. But tell your aunt all about your father, for I can see she's longing to hear."

"Oh, Aunt Clare, I'm sorry!" cried Ilonka. "It's just that I was so surprised to find that Magnolia is Lizzie."

"I *thought* you'd be nice company for her during the holidays," said Mrs. Lenning with a satisfied smile.

# ADVENTURE IN GEOGRAPHY

### By GWEN THORNBER

"THE great Pitch Lake of Trinidad," said Miss Matthews brightly, "is one hundred and fourteen acres in extent and every year produces thousands of tons of asphalt, believed to be a carboniferous deposit formed from petroleum escaped from the oil-sands beneath."

Judy stifled a sigh, idly drawing ballet dancers on the back of her rough-note book. Who cared about the Pitch Lake, anyway, or the whole of Trinidad for that matter, even if Daddy did have business connections with the oilfields! Who cared about the entire bunch of West Indies—a tiresome group of islands that were difficult to draw, in a sea that was a teaser to spell!

A paper pellet landed on her desk and she looked up to meet the bored eyes of Pam Heywood, who hated geography as much as Judy did herself. Grinning, she took a scrap of paper and scribbled on it a parody of the song which they had just been trolling lustily in singing class.

"I've never seen the Amazon,
I've never reached Brazil,
But Miss Matthews and Miss MacAndrew
They can go there when they will.
And if they think these places
Are so glorious to behold,
Then I wish they'd go to Rio,
Go rolling down to Rio,
Yes, I wish they'd go to Rio
And stay there till they're old."

It wasn't a very brilliant effort, but it made Pam chuckle when she received the paper, folded into an arrow and flicked onto her desk with the skill born of long practice. She returned it with a composition of her own on the back, and Judy was perusing it when she became aware of a curious stillness in the room. Glancing up, she realised that Miss Matthews had stopped the lesson and was regarding her in silence.

"Well, Judith," she said at last with mock sweetness, "are you already acquainted with what I am telling the class?"

"N-no, Miss Matthews," stammered Judy.

"Then I'm afraid I must ask you to attend detention on Friday afternoon, to learn the work you have failed to do in class."

Judy sat down, while a little groan ran round the class. Her abundant energy went into games, not work, and her detention would rob the Lower Fourth of its best centre forward in the match against the Fifth.

"Oh, Judy!" moaned Pam as they left the classroom. "Don't get any more detentions or you may miss the match against Lanston House."

"I'd like to sink Mattie in her precious Pitch Lake!" fumed Gillian Lawrence. "Smiling sweetly while she gives you the punishment she knows you mind most!"

"Still, it's my own fault," admitted Judy. "But I'll try to be more careful. Only somehow——"

She did not finish her sentence. It was hard to explain the excited feeling which bubbled up inside her when she got among other girls, the feeling that made her want to laugh and romp and enjoy herself. Perhaps it was because life at home was pretty dull, with Daddy's Aunt Susan keeping house since Mummy died, and no young people in the village. Daddy, of course, was a dear, with his kindly humour, his affectionate understanding, but when Judy, a weekly boarder, went back to school on Monday mornings, she always felt as though she'd a lot of steam to let off. And in letting it off she sometimes got into trouble.

The lesson after break was French, another subject Judy detested. But she wrestled earnestly with the mysteries of personal pronouns, until the sound of her own name made her look up, to see a prefect standing by the mistress's desk.

"Judith Lyle," said Mademoiselle, "Miss MacAndrew wishes to see you in the study."

Judy rose slowly to her feet, conscious of her form-mates' dismay. Had Miss Matthews reported her, or had some other peccadillo been brought to the Head's notice? There was that practical joke on the prefects—and the midnight feast in the dormitory. Still, she hadn't been the only one. . . . Nervously she tapped at the study door.

"Come in!" called the Head's brusque Scottish voice.

Judy opened the door and stepped inside. Then she saw that Miss MacAndrew was not alone. A man was sitting in the big chair by the fire, and her cry of delighted recognition died away in a gasp of horror. Had the Head sent for Daddy?

"Judy!" He came forward to kiss her and she saw with unutterable relief that he was smiling. "Why, what's the matter, darling? You've gone as white as a sheet!"

"It—it was such a surprise," faltered Judy.

"I'm sure it was," agreed Miss MacAndrew, and Judy glanced at her quickly, wondering if she imagined that twinkle of sardonic amusement in the headmistress's eyes. "Well, I have a class waiting for me, Mr. Lyle, so I will leave you and your daughter together."

"Well, Judy," said Mr. Lyle as the door closed, "I am glad to hear from Miss MacAndrew that you're doing so well at gym and games. I wish," he added reluctantly, "that she could give me as good an account of your work and conduct."

"I'm sorry," murmured Judy.

"It is for that reason," went on her father, "that she is rather reluctant to agree to the project I have in mind—a project which would involve your missing the rest of this term's work."

"Oh, Daddy," cried Judy, "what is it?"

"Nothing less than a trip to Trinidad with me."

"O-oh!" Judy gasped with delight. Trinidad might be a dull place, but she would have the voyage and the thrill of seeing things that the other girls had never seen.

"It's this way," her father was explaining. "The firm is sending me there on a special job, and I thought it would be an enjoyable experience for you and help you to realise that there's more in life than chasing a ball or climbing ropes. Miss MacAndrew, I may say, doesn't see eye to eye with me."

"But she won't stop me?"

"No, she agrees that the decision must rest with me. I've promised to fly back so that you'll be in time for the beginning of next term. Now, run and get packed, for I'm taking you home today."

A week later, Judy found herself standing on the station platform very conscious of her suitcase labelled "S. S. CASSANDRA, TRINIDAD" in big red letters.

"I'll keep these labels always," she told her father. "Why, I thought it was wonderful for Diana Jervis to have 'Paris' on her case, but Trinidad is miles further than Paris."

"Over three thousand miles," agreed Mr. Lyle, smiling.

When they reached the docks, Judy gave a cry of excitement as she caught sight of a great liner towering over the customs sheds and ware-houses.

"Oh," she gasped, "is that the *Cassandra*?"

"No," laughed her father. "That's the *Queen Elizabeth*. There's our ship!"

"Oh!" said Judy again, but in a different tone. Beside the great bulk of the *Queen Elizabeth*, the *Cassandra* looked far too small to cross those miles of tossing ocean.

But once aboard, she found that it was quite a large ship. She was still exploring when a throbbing noise began, and a voice boomed through a megaphone: "Attention, please! Attention, please! Will all visitors go ashore, as the ship is now about to sail."

Judy ran on deck, to find gangways being lifted and ropes cast off. Then, overhead, she heard the strangest, most thrilling sound of her life—the siren of a ship about to sail. A few minutes later the *Cassandra* slid quietly away from her moorings and the voyage had begun.

On the second day out they had what the officers called a "stiff swell", but Judy was not sick, though there were many empty places in the dining-saloon. By the sixth day the sea had grown calm and the winds had lost their sting. Judy, seeing passengers lining the rails, slipped into a vacant place beside her father.

"What are they looking for?" she asked him.

"The Azores."

Judy wrinkled her brow. She'd heard of the Azores—what was it? "At Flores in the Azores Sir Richard Grenville lay." So this was where the little *Revenge* had fought her last fight! And then there was Columbus, whose ships must have sailed these same waters! Oh, if only she knew more about him, so that she could imagine what it felt like to be on the little sailing-ship *Santa Maria*, adventuring into the unknown, instead of on the s.s. *Cassandra*, bound for a safe port across well-charted seas!

Soon the sun shone in a cloudless sky, and Judy, in the middle of December, went into cotton frocks. She saw her first flying-fish, skimming

I-B-G—C

over the waves like tiny birds, and a school of dolphins leaping in and out of the water. And one morning she went up early on deck to see a range of mountains towering into the clouds.

"South America," someone told her. "We're approaching Trinidad."

"South America!" So those were the squiggles Miss Matthews chalked on the blackboard!

They sailed past the chain of islands or Bocas which guarded the approach to Port-of-Spain, and saw more mountains rising over the roofs of the port, tree-clad peaks green against a blue sky. And Judy, whose fourteen years had been lived on the flats of East Anglia, thrilled to their challenge, their mystery.

As they drove through the streets of the town she leant out of the window, fascinated by the crowds that thronged the streets—white people with tanned or sallow skins, Indians, Chinese, African negroes.

"Oh, Daddy, I can't wait to see more of Trinidad!" she exclaimed. "Where do we go tomorrow?"

"Well," returned her father, "I've got to hire a car and do some business at one of the oilfields, so we'll do the correct thing and go on to the Pitch Lake."

The drive to the Lake was more interesting than Judy had expected. They drove through villages of African huts nestling among bread-fruit and banana trees, swampy ricefields, and plains of waving sugar-cane. Then they reached the oil-belt, with its tanks and factories, and finally came to the oilfield connected with Daddy's firm. Here, while he talked business, the manager's wife took Judy for a bathe in a deliciously warm sea, and afterwards gave them tea at her bungalow before they drove on to the Pitch Lake.

The Lake, at first sight, was even duller than Judy had anticipated—a stretch of what looked like sun-dried mud, broken by channels of dirty water. But when she stood on its hot, yielding surface and talked to the men who worked there, she began to feel a little of their awe for what the guide-book called "this wonder of the world".

"It's like the widow's cruse," she remarked to her father. "You take some out of it and by morning it's filled up again."

"Yes, and I wish I had some shares in it," returned Mr. Lyle feelingly. "But now I think we'd better be making tracks if we don't want to miss dinner. That handsome Indian waiter hinted that there would be guava ice-cream on tonight's menu."

"We mustn't miss that," agreed Judy as they walked to the car. "Oh, Daddy, Trinidad's *fun!*"

She gave a little skip from sheer light-heartedness, and then became aware of a pair of lustrous dark eyes regarding her with a rather superior stare. Judy stopped skipping and stared back. The eyes belonged to quite the most beautiful girl she had ever seen. She was, Judy decided, about seventeen, slim and graceful, with glossy black hair elaborately waved. Her features were delicate, her skin of a creamy pallor, and her lovely, rather sullen mouth was painted a deep crimson. She wore an immaculate white linen dress, trimmed with exquisite drawn-thread embroidery, high-heeled white shoes, and a gold filigree brooch and bracelets.

"Come on, Judy!" called her father, and she took her place in the car. He started the engine and pressed the accelerator, but, instead of moving, the car remained motionless, as though a gigantic hand was holding it in place. Mr. Lyle tried again, and then got out to investigate.

"Good lord!" he exclaimed. "The car's sunk into the road."

A sudden ripple of laughter made them both look up. The dark girl had come up behind them and was contemplating their plight with undisguised amusement. Judy flushed indignantly, and the girl instantly composed her face.

"I'm sorry, but you looked so surprised!"

"We are," retorted Mr. Lyle. "In England, we're accustomed to roads that will bear the weight of a car."

"So you're English!" The girl spoke in a soft, nasal drawl with which Judy was becoming familiar. "My dad's of English extraction but my mother was Spanish. Here's Dad now!"

"Well, you sure are in a mess!" said a voice with a strong Trinidad accent. "Someone should have told you to find a hard patch to park your car. In places the roadside is almost as soft as the Lake. Here you!" he called to a couple of negroes standing near. "Come and lend a hand!"

They all pushed and heaved, but without avail.

"Guess I'd better give you a tow," said their new acquaintance. "Can you chaps get a rope?"

The rope was brought and the Lyles' car attached to that of the stranger. Helped by a number of workers who pushed behind, their new friend's limousine drew it onto firmer ground.

"I'm extremely grateful to you," said Mr. Lyle, presenting his card. "I only wish I could do something for you in return."

"Wait a bit," said their rescuer thoughtfully, as he slipped an arm round his daughter's shoulders. "I'm not so sure that you can't. Are you in a hurry?"

Mr. Lyle glanced at his watch. "I'm afraid not," he replied. "We couldn't be back in time for dinner now."

"Fine! You can have dinner with me. There's a country club outside San Fernando where they do pretty well, and I suggest you wait for explanations till we get there."

Later, across the dinner table, he looked earnestly at Mr. Lyle.

"Guess you're wondering what the mystery is. Well, I'm Doug Tennant, owner of a sugar plantation. We've got a strike on just now, fomented by a particularly dangerous agitator who calls himself 'the Corbeau', after our Trinidad bird which looks and behaves like a vulture. Years ago I was instrumental in getting him a gaol sentence, so his grudge against me is personal as well as political. In fact"—he glanced uneasily at his daughter—"a chap I met just now was warning me that the Corbeau may try to get at me through Sonia. Now maybe I don't know you, but I can see the type of folk you are, and I want to ask if you'll take her back to your hotel and look after her for a few days. Then I can fight the Corbeau with an easy mind."

"With pleasure," said Mr. Lyle. "It will be nice for Judy to have a companion. How old is Sonia?"

"Fifteen," returned her father, "though I guess she looks more. Girls grow up fast out here."

"Only fifteen!" said Judy to herself. "And she uses lipstick and nail varnish! I wish Miss MacAndrew could see her!"

So it came about that Judy returned to the hotel with a companion. At first, reluctance to leave her father made Sonia moody and silent, but gradually she began to respond to the friendliness of her hosts. Her sophisticated manner made Judy feel very childish, but she soon discovered that Sonia was interested and amused by her accounts of school life and escapades in England. Sonia's own school life, at a small convent, sounded dull by comparison, though outside school she had done things that filled Judy with envy. She had been to grown-up dances, belonged to grown-up clubs, and even flown to America.

"Perhaps there'll be a dance while you're here," she told Judy. "Anyway, you must see plenty of Trinidad. Let's get your father to drive us to the mountains today."

But when Judy opened her father's door to see why he was late for breakfast she found him still in bed, his face flushed with fever. The doctor, hastily summoned, pronounced it a mild attack of malaria, and Judy spent the next few days helping Mrs. Hutchins, the capable proprietress, to nurse him. Not till he was sitting up in his room would she listen to the doctor's words of wisdom.

"Get that pretty friend of yours to take you out into the country. Hanging over a sick bed has taken all the roses out of your cheeks."

"He's quite right," urged Sonia. "Let's get a taxi and drive somewhere nice. We might take a picnic to the Blue Basin and bathe there."

"That would be lovely," agreed Judy. "It's so hot!"

"Then it's settled," pronounced Mrs. Hutchins. "I'll get the servants to pack you a nice picnic tea." She turned away, and Judy leant over the parapet, watching the traffic.

"Look, Sonia!" she exclaimed suddenly. "That chocolate-coloured car looks like a taxi waiting for passengers. It's been there since before lunch. I'll ask him what he'd charge."

She ran down the steps and across the road.

"Could you take my friend and me for a picnic to the Blue Basin?"

The coloured driver looked at her, and then at Sonia, leaning gracefully on the parapet.

"Yes, please." He spoke eagerly, as though glad of a fare.

"And what would you charge? We should want you to wait an hour or two."

"Two dollars."

"Thank you. I'll speak to my friend."

She ran back to the terrace just as Mrs. Hutchins emerged from the house.

"I've spoken to the garage I always employ," the proprietress announced, "and they're sending Beckles, their most reliable driver, to take you and wait for you for four dollars."

"But that man across the road only wants two dollars!" cried Judy.

"Must be a 'pirate' taxi, then," said Mrs. Hutchins. "No, my dear, when you're abroad always get your taxis from a recognised place. Four dollars is pretty cheap."

The taxi arrived and, complete with picnic basket and bathing clothes, they drove into the hilly country behind the town. They left the car at the foot of a steep, wooded hill and climbed a path winding between trees and shrubs. Here were cocoa and coffee bushes, bananas and breadfruit, pawpaws and coconuts. Now and again they paused to look across the valley, where flame-coloured immortelle trees made a splash of vivid colour against the green, or watched the lizards darting across the path or the humming-birds hovering over the flowers.

At last they heard the music of running water, and saw before them the Blue Basin, a small lake lying in the shadow of a cliff down which a waterfall sprang from the midst of dense tropical foliage.

"Oh, how lovely!" exclaimed Judy. "I'm dying to plunge in and get cool."

"There's the bathing-hut!" Sonia indicated a small wooden building. "But wouldn't you like your tea first?"

"It would be rather nice," agreed Judy.

They ate their tea in the shade of a mahogany tree, and then pushed their utensils back into the basket. Afterwards they undressed and plunged into the waters of the lake.

The shadows were lengthening before either of them thought of the passage of time. Then Sonia spoke.

"Coming out, Judy?"

"Oh, not yet!" Judy lay on her back, floating and gazing up at the cool green of the trees. "It's so lovely here!"

"All right, I'll go and dress first."

Sonia took a long time dressing, and when she emerged, immaculate as ever, Judy was ready to leave the water. She ran into the hut, leaving Sonia seated on a stone by the pool reading a magazine.

Blue veils of dusk lay over the valley when Judy emerged from the hut. She fastened the door behind her, and then turned towards the spot where she had left Sonia. But Sonia was not there. Her bathing clothes lay by the stone with her magazine, but she herself had vanished.

Puzzled, Judy looked around, calling Sonia's name, and then walked a few yards down the track, wondering if she had wandered off in search of flowers. But there was no sign of her, and the tropical nightfall was at hand.

Judy called again and again, but only the echoes answered her. Then, with a growing sense of panic, she raced down the path to the car. The driver lay huddled in his seat, asleep.

"Beckles!" She shook him by the shoulder. "Beckles, wake up!"

He opened his dark eyes and then sat up.

"Coming back, missie?"

"No, I can't find my friend. Have you seen her?"

He shook his curly head.

"She's hiding, maybe."

"She wouldn't do a silly thing like that, especially when it's getting so late. Oh, I'm afraid something must have happened to her!"

"But what could have happened?" He began to climb out of the car. "When did you miss her?"

Judy told him what had happened as they walked up the path to the Basin. Together they searched round the pool, calling and shouting, but there was still no sign of the missing girl.

Beckles shook his head in bewilderment.

"Doan' understand it—unless she got someone to take her home."

"She wouldn't leave me like that, and, anyway, there was no one to take her."

"A car came past just after we all got here, and a chap got out and then the car went on. Big chocolate-coloured car."

"A chocolate-coloured car!" A strange fear caught at Judy's heart. "Oh, Beckles, I don't quite understand, but I'm sure there's something wrong. We must get help."

Together they hurried down the steep path, stumbling over the uneven ground. When they reached the car Beckles opened the door for Judy, but she paused with one foot on the step, looking back at the dark, lonely valley. Somewhere in that gathering darkness Sonia might still be hidden, helpless in the power of an unknown enemy. If they went and left her would they ever find her again?

"Beckles," whispered Judy, "you must go back without me. I'm staying here."

"Staying here? You can't, missie!"

"Yes, I can. I'll hide among the bushes and no one will know I'm here, but if anything happens I can tell you when you get back."

"But your folk—what will they say?"

"Tell Mrs. Hutchins not to let Daddy know if she can help it. Go now, quickly, and as soon as you get to a phone ring up the police and the hotel. Then come back to me."

The car moved slowly forward, its headlamps making a pathway of light along the dark path. Then it was gone, and Judy was left alone in the warm darkness.

She shrank back into a clump of bushes, trembling. Around her a continual chorus of soft squeaks and hums and rustlings bore witness to the myriad little creatures moving to and fro in the darkness. A mosquito stung her cheek, and she recalled with a shudder that there were snakes and poisonous insects in Trinidad. Once something ran over her foot and she nearly screamed aloud. But somehow she kept her head, realising with a sense of wry amusement that she was in the sort of situation in which she, like most girl guides, had often dreamed of finding herself—a situation testing all her courage, observation, and initiative. Well, the reality wasn't quite so exciting as the story-books suggested, but she'd got to stick it out for Sonia's sake.

Suddenly a new sound fell on her ears, the low hum of an engine, and her heart leaped with relief. Could this be Beckles back already with help? But no, the sound came from the wrong direction.

A moment later, powerful headlamps lit up the road below her as a big car swung round a bend and drew up at the foot of the path leading to the Basin. Judy stood quite still while the driver sounded his horn three times. In answer, a long low whistle shrilled down the valley, and a few minutes later she heard the sound of feet scraping on the stones higher up the path. Then into the circle of light cast by the headlamps came a big negro, carrying in his arms a girl in a white dress.

Sonia's face was turned away, but Judy could see that she had a scarf over her mouth and her hands tied behind her back. The negro laid her on the floor of the car, and then seated himself beside the driver.

As he slammed the door Judy ran softly forward and turned the handle of the luggage boot. It opened, and as the engine began to purr she scrambled into the empty boot and crouched there, holding onto the edge, while the car moved slowly forward.

It gathered speed and soon was racing along the dark highway with the light of street lamps and houses flashing by. Presently the lights became more numerous and Judy guessed that they were on the outskirts of Port-of-Spain. There was more traffic on the roads now, but their pace did not slacken until they drew up at a cross-roads, one of a line of cars held up by a policeman.

Judy poked her head round the edge of her hiding-place. There were two vehicles in front of them and a bus had stopped just behind. No, there wasn't room for the chocolate-coloured car to get out of the line.

Quickly Judy scrambled to the ground and raced across to the policeman.

"Stop that car!" she cried. "They're kidnapping a girl!"

He looked at her incredulously.

"Please!" she implored him. "Don't let them get away!"

Without a word, he held up a majestic hand to immobilise the traffic and then, with Judy beside him, walked over to the chocolate-coloured car. But before they reached it a door on the other side opened and two men tumbled out and raced away down the road.

The policeman blew his whistle, another whistle answered it, and shouts and cries resounded down the street. But Judy did not heed them. She was kneeling by Sonia, untying her hands, removing the scarf from her mouth. . . .

"I was sitting reading by the pool," Sonia told them later as she lay in bed at the hotel, "when a coat or something was thrown over my head, and I was picked up and carried into the woods. I tried to scream, but I couldn't. I was terrified. And if it hadn't been for Judy I'd probably have been in their hands still. By the time Beckles got the police on their track they'd have had me hidden away somewhere."

"And with you as a hostage, the Corbeau would have expected me to throw in my hand," added her father, who had been summoned by phone from his plantation. "Guess I would have, too." He turned to Judy. "Are you sure you'd recognise the driver of the car?"

"Yes," returned Judy. "He had sleek black hair, a hook nose, and dark eyes with a yellow spot in the—yes, the left one."

"That's the Corbeau all right," said Mr. Tennant. "We'll have him if he doesn't get off the island; and if he does, Trinidad will be well rid of him. But even so——"

He paused, looking thoughtfully from one girl to another.

"Even without him, the labour situation won't be settled. There may be more strikes on the plantation—even riots—and after the scare I've had tonight I'd like to feel Sonia was out of it all. That's why I've been putting a proposition to Mr. Lyle."

"What?" asked Judy and Sonia together.

"Well, I've said that I'd like Sonia to go back to Judy's school if he would have her as a boarder at week-ends and holidays. And I'm glad to say he's agreed."

"Oh, how marvellous!" cried Judy. "Sonia, you *would* like it, wouldn't you?"

"Yes," said Sonia promptly. "I shan't like leaving Father, but I'd love to go home with you, Judy."

"You'll love England, too," said Mrs. Hutchins, entering with a tray of coffee. "Do you know anything about it?"

"Only from the geography book," replied Sonia with distaste. "'The British Isles lie between latitude 50 and 60 degrees North and longitude o and 10 degrees West.' 'The Pennine Hills are formed from three layers of rock—(*a*) mountain limestone, (*b*) millstone grit, and (*c*) coal measures.' 'The Port of London——'"

"Wait a minute!" interrupted Judy. "I'll get my book of holiday snaps."

She ran off, returning with a large album into which she had already pasted some photos of Trinidad.

"Look!" she said to Sonia. "Here is a mountain that Daddy and I climbed."

"How thrilling!" breathed Sonia. "Those great rocky crags, and that peak against the sky!"

"The Pennine Hills," murmured Judy, "in three layers, mountain limestone, millstone grit, and——"

Sonia heaved a pillow at her. "Shut up," she commanded, "and tell me more about these lovely places! Where are these enchanting thatched cottages, and this great river with all the pleasure craft?"

"That's a lane in Devon, and this is Marlow on the Thames. And here's London Bridge. Oh, Sonia, you've been thinking of England as I used to think of Trinidad—just a lot of meaningless names in a book! But now——"

She fell silent, lost in her own thoughts. Trinidad had given her Sonia, a friend to share home life as well as school, and it had given her, too, a wealth of memories—mountains green against a blue sky, palm groves and canefields, humming birds and flying fish, and white teeth glinting in laughing, dusky faces. There must be beauty and adventure and romance, strange and lovely sights and sounds, in all those other places that had just been names in a book. . . .

"Oh, Sonia," she said earnestly, "that's what geography is for—to give you a sort of chart of places you will someday discover for yourself—to help you to find the way and understand what you see! Perhaps that's the point of other lessons, too."

"I guess you're right," said Sonia.

# WANTED—A FRIEND

## By BARBARA HECTOR

PAMELA WILSON glowered at the calendar which was set to show the month of April, then, smiling triumphantly, she drew a thick, black pencil stroke through the first week. She surveyed her handiwork with satisfaction, then scrabbled in her pencil-box and put a crimson crown above a certain date, the day school was to close for the Easter holidays.

"So that's the way you feel about it, dear!"

Pam was startled. She had thought herself quite alone in her new attic bedroom. She had left the door wide open, and now as she turned to greet her grannie she saw that the old lady carried a laden tray.

"I thought tea together on your window seat would be delightful, Pam. Do you mind me intruding?" Mrs. Wilson asked tentatively.

"It's a lovely idea!" Pam enthused and rushed to arrange the cushions and to draw up a wicker table.

When they were both settled, Grannie Wilson returned to the topic she had first touched upon.

"Coming to a new place is always difficult, dear. And going to a new school in term-time is quite hateful, I suppose," she consoled. Then sighing, "It will pass," she predicted.

"It's taking such a time in passing," Pam complained. "I suppose really it's due to the fact that I'm the thirteenth girl in the class and very much the odd girl out. Everyone is paired off with someone else. No one ever seems to notice me—except the teacher."

She paused thoughtfully and then corrected herself.

"There's a girl absent just now. She's been off ill all the term. Her name is Rose Harding. She sounds awfully nice. Next term, when she comes back, things may be better. At least I'll have someone to sit beside. The desks are twosome."

"I'm sure it will be better next term." Grannie spoke brightly.

"But perhaps they'll go on not noticing me," Pam remarked. "This Rose is a wonderful girl. She seems to do everything well: skate, play tennis, she swims and she dances. I—I'm so unnoticeable, Gran."

"You need *a handle*!" The old lady chuckled.

"A handle?" Pam was mystified.

"It's a phrase, dear. A handle to your name! You're not noticed because you are very normal, very ordinary. Which is quite an advantage sometimes. But it would be nice to be *the girl who sings* or *the girl with golden hair*." Gran lowered her voice. "I was a very ordinary girl when I was young."

"A handle to my name," Pam mused, but she could think of none. How she wished she had some distinguishing ability.

On Monday morning, when she was ready to set off for school, she peeped out round an edge of the curtain and drew back hurriedly.

"I'm looking to see if the coast is clear," she explained. "The girl next door, Betsy Squire, crosses the road right away, I think *to avoid me*."

"But how unkind!" Mrs. Wilson exclaimed.

"It isn't really, Gran. She meets her chum at the corner. Naturally they don't want me to walk with them. They have their secrets. She's coming now." Pam backed from the window. "She's coming up our path!" She marvelled.

"A gesture of welcome at last for the new girl, Pam. How very kind. Shall I go to the door?" the old lady suggested. And, "I could say something—er—tactful and then call to you to come."

"Please, Gran. That would be nice." Pam's heart was beating excitedly. Perhaps she had been wrong about Betsy having a chum. Perhaps Betsy wanted her, Pam, as a special friend.

Mrs. Wilson passed into the hall and swung the door wide.

"Good morning, dear. I saw you coming up the path," she began.

Betsy's eyes were wide with apprehension, her face unsmiling.

"The postman put *your* letters into *our* box." Briskly Betsy handed them over to the astonished Mrs. Wilson, turned and ran down the steps. "I'm in a dreadful hurry," she called back over her shoulder as if in explanation.

Gran and Pam eyed each other curiously.

"Well really!" Mrs. Wilson gasped.

"That's the way it is." Pam looked resigned. And then asked, "Any for me?"

"I haven't my glasses." Mrs. Wilson handed the letters over.

"One for Daddy," Pam reported. "One for you from Uncle Alec and——" Pam was speechless for a moment. "There's one for me marked *From the Brighton Police* on the economy label." Her voice was a mere, awe-struck whisper while through her brain darted frantic, terrifying questions.

What crime had she ever committed?

How had the police got her name?

"The brooch you found that day we spent in Brighton three months ago!" Gran remembered to Pam's relief. "When you handed it to a policeman you were asked for your name and address."

"Of course!" Pam exulted. "The letter's been forwarded from home —our old home. How silly to forget about it." She slit the envelope and read the short communication. "The brooch hasn't been claimed, Gran. So I'm to receive it, if I call or—or I've to send instructions."

"We'll go to Brighton for the day on Saturday, child." Mrs. Wilson smiled on Pam. "Something to look forward to all through your dreary schooldays!"

Delighted, Pam rushed off, but, seeing a group of schoolgirls at the corner, she ceased skipping along, she smoothed the smile from her face and sobered her joyous feelings.

An outing to the sea wasn't much fun when you couldn't share it with another girl, when you had no chum with whom to talk over your good news. And the brooch? It was lovely. A plain gold pin with a pink pearl near one end of it. It was quite suitable for Pam, but—who would admire it at school? No one would congratulate her on her good fortune.

Shyly she looked in the direction of her new schoolmates, prepared to force a smile on to her lips. Instead she felt as if ice gathered on her spine, her unborn smile froze.

Betsy was in the centre of the group, obviously dishing up for her friends a juicy bit of gossip.

Pam's heart lurched sickeningly.

Betsy was telling them about Pam's letter! *From the Brighton Police.*

Pam's first impulse was to join the group and gaily show them the letter. She could say, " You're quite right, Betsy, to warn your friends that I *may* be disreputable. But—read my letter and see for yourselves!"

Pam frowned. No! She would not do that. Unnoticed, she sped past the knot of schoolgirls. She would keep her letter to herself. She would show it at once if anyone tackled her about it. Just as she had jumped to the wrong conclusion when first she saw the letter, so had Betsy, and Betsy was spreading the information. And although probably the girls would consider the possibility that Pam's communication was innocent enough—she might have ignored a halt sign when cycling or she might have witnessed an accident—they, too, might suspect Pam of having been involved in—well, something unsavoury! It was time Betsy and her pals learned to question before they condemned!

Pam could have laughed. She had received what she had wanted— *a handle to her name!*

She was the girl who had had a letter from the Brighton police— or worse! Imagination, like elastic, can stretch to extraordinary lengths.

If Pam had been unnoticed before, now she was the most noticed girl in the school. Heads turned in her direction. Talk ceased on her approach. No one, save teachers, spoke to her. Girls looked at her from under lowered lashes, wonderingly, others suspiciously, some condemningly.

Pam forced herself to look serene and uncaring, but it was terribly difficult. She longed to flaunt her letter before the class, but no one gave her an opening.

"I'll never be able to tell them, to clear myself," she thought darkly.

The week, and the term, dragged to a close, the matter unexplained, the girls still coldly suspicious.

Saturday, as if to make up, dawned gloriously. Pam's father drove his mother and daughter to the junction. The train was drawing into the

station as they arrived, but they found seats at last and sank down gratefully.

"What a rush!" Mrs. Wilson exclaimed as the train started. And then, "Did you remember the letter, Pam? It said you had to bring it with you —to the Lost Property Office, as a reference."

"It's here." Pam took off her new blue felt school hat, and the letter tumbled on to her lap, from there to the floor.

Its economy label twinkled up at her.

I-B-G—D

*From the Brighton Police.*

"Now everyone will think me an escaped convict!" she burbled as she stooped to pick it up.

But the girl sitting opposite her, a girl she hadn't noticed, was quicker.

"Are you Pam Wilson, the new girl at school?" this girl asked. "I'm Rose Harding. Mother"—she indicated the lady beside her— "is taking me to Brighton to get over my illness. Do tell me! I—I couldn't help hearing what—what was said. Are you foxing the form? Letting them think—what they think? What a joke!"

Pam explained and soon Mrs. Wilson and Mrs. Harding were chatting like old friends, as were the two girls.

"We'll spend the afternoon together, Pam," Rose suggested. And, "You've been so sporty over this, I'm sure we'll be friends."

"You're terribly popular in the form, Rose," Pam confided. "The girls are always talking of you and the wonderful things you do."

"Rot!" Rose laughed. "I'm goodish at games, but I'm a duffer at lessons. Still—I'm glad they like me. I like them. We're chary of strangers." She scowled thoughtfully. Then, "I haven't had a chum, Pam, since Carol Dunn left last term."

Her gaze met Pam's, enquiring, frank and then confident.

"I'll tell them about the letter," Rose promised. "The first day of term!"

And Pam knew that she had found a friend.

———————

# The Last Day of the Holidays

## By CHARLOTTE M. KELLY

"BUT of course we will be delighted to see you! Four o'clock then. Goodbye." Mrs. Bartley put down the telephone and said over her shoulder: "Mrs. Rowlandson is coming to tea this afternoon, Jean."

The girl who had been writing letters at the table looked up with a frown. "Mummie, my last day! How annoying! Couldn't you put her off? It's not as if the Rowlandsons were great friends of ours. They've only been in this den a month."

"Exactly," her mother responded. "It's because Mrs. Rowlandson is almost a stranger to me that I can't put her off, as I would if I knew her better. She wants to talk to me about some of the poor people in the village. You'll like her. I thought her charming the day I called at the manor."

Jean's lips tightened in the obstinate way her mother dreaded. "Well, I'm going to take Tigger for a long walk," she announced. "I *may* be home for tea."

"Oh, Jean!" protested Mrs. Bartley. "I want you to be here. She's bringing her little girl with her. Her name is Stephanie and she's just twelve."

"Spoilt little brat, I expect," muttered Jean. She had not the slightest desire to meet the new owners of Thisden Grange, who were reputed to be very wealthy and extremely devoted to their only child. Besides, this was her last chance of a good tramp until Christmas and she wasn't going to miss it for a dozen Stephanie Rowlandsons. So, despite her mother's disapproval, and the rain that was falling in a steady downpour, she set out after lunch, the black-and-white terrier at her heels.

51

"Remember Daddy will be home early to drive you to the station at six o'clock," her mother warned her. "But do come back soon. That poor child will be so bored with no one young here."

"I'll try," promised Jean half-heartedly. The feelings of the visitors did not concern her in the slightest, but she knew that her father, a busy doctor, would make a point of coming home to tea that afternoon so that they could all be together on the last day of her holidays. Later that evening she was going up to town to spend the night with Dr. Bartley's sister, and at nine o'clock next morning she would take her place among the entrants for the Forsyth Shield. This Shield, competed for annually by one pupil from every school in the Home Counties, was the gift of a distinguished literary man, and it was considered a great honour to win it. St. Damian's, Jean's school, had never achieved this honour; so when Jean, to her mingled embarrassment and delight, had been chosen to represent the school this year she determined to do her very best to justify the choice. During the summer holidays now ending she had passed hours reading the prose masters "for style", the only preparation she could make, since the competition consisted of an essay, the subject of which would not be made known beforehand. Jean had a natural facility for expressing herself, but she had her bad patches and was pursued now by the fear that when the time came she might "dry up".

There was a strong wind blowing as she and Tigger left the square white house known to the villagers as "t'doctor's" and to the Bartleys' friends as "Lyndon". Plodding along the sloping road that led to Thisden Hill, with the rain beating on her face, and her shoes squelching up and down in the mud, Jean began to regret her foolhardiness in coming out on such a day. She regretted it still more as she struggled, panting, to the top of the hill, where the wind almost took her breath away. From this point on a fine day she could see for miles in every direction, but this afternoon a mist obscured the view and the rain fell relentlessly. What an idiot she was to have left the house, she reflected gloomily, as after a brief rest in the shelter of the rocks that crowned the Hill she began her journey back. But she could not have stayed at home. In her present state of mind it would have been agony to spend the afternoon making polite conversation with strangers. If only her mind didn't go blank tomorrow! The more she thought, the more convinced Jean was that St. Damian's should have chosen someone else to compete for the Shield. Stella Crean, perhaps, who had got the prize for English Literature last year. Or Mary West, who had actually written a play that was going to be performed by the Dramatic Society at Christmas. Anyone but herself.

The failing light made her look at her watch. It was later than she thought, so she decided to take a short cut through the woods, though even then she would not be home in time for tea. That could not be helped, but she must not miss her train. The wind that was now behind her blew her more rapidly down the hill than was really comfortable, so when she got to the edge of the woods she stopped to get her breath. But not for long. Tigger had a passion for chasing real or imaginary rabbits and had to be carefully watched or he would disappear for hours.

Entering the wood was like plunging into a dark tunnel. She could barely distinguish the path before her. There was no sound but the soughing of wind in the trees above and the angry rush of the waters in the river, flooded from a week of rain. Jean loved the river in all its moods, but now she hesitated, tempted by the darkness to keep to the upper path. But that was longer and she was anxious to get home as soon as she could. With Tigger slipping and slithering in the mud, she made her way down to the river. Brown turgid water raced swiftly between the banks, overflowing the path at one point so that Jean had to circle through the soaked undergrowth to get on. She stumbled along, not lifting her eyes from the ground until the sound of a voice made her pause. A small white figure loomed out of the dusk a few yards away. For an instant all the ghost stories she had read flashed through her mind, but then she realised that this was no ghost but a girl in a gleaming white waterproof. She had a plump childish face and dark curly hair on which the raindrops sparkled, and she sat huddled up on the trunk of a tree blown down the previous winter.

"What's the matter? Why are you sitting there in the rain?" asked Jean with quick sympathy.

"Because I can't do anything else!" replied the child in an aggrieved tone. "I slipped in the mud and hurt my foot. My ankle is frightfully sore and—and I've been here for *hours*!" Her voice began to shake. "I hate the dark. Don't go away and leave me."

"But we can't stay here," protested Jean. "Lean on me and see if you can walk. That's it!" But a few steps convinced her that they could make no progress that way.

"I'll have to get help," she declared. "What's your name, and where do you live?"

"I'm Stephanie Rowlandson and I live at Thisden Grange."

"Oh! Well, my name is Jean Bartley. But what made you come down here this evening?" asked Jean, reflecting that she was not the only lunatic in the world.

"I ran away," the child confessed. "Mummie was taking me to visit some people and I didn't want to go. I hate visiting!"

"Indeed." Jean suppressed the impulse to retort that *she* hated being visited and said instead: "It is at our house that your mother is spending the afternoon. Now I must go."

But at that Stephanie protested vigorously. She wept stormily and implored of Jean not to leave her.

"Don't you see that I must?" Jean explained as patiently as she could. "I won't be long. I'll get Daddy to come and drive you home, or if your mother is still with us you can come to her. And Tigger can keep you company while I'm away."

But Tigger had his own views on the matter and Jean had not gone a hundred yards before she found him trotting beside her with a defiant cock of his tail. Well, Stephanie would just have to put up with it. For a girl of twelve she was absurdly babyish.

Jean reached the road and ran home to Lyndon as fast as she could. It was too dark to see her watch, but she knew that it would take her all her time to bring help to Stephanie and then catch her own train. By skipping supper she might just do it. There was no sign of the doctor's car as she came panting up the avenue, but her mother's little Morris stood there, side by side with a long gleaming car.

She went straight to the drawing-room, where she found Mrs. Bartley with her visitors, a small white-faced woman and a stout man.

"Mummie, where's Daddy? I'm in an awful hurry!"

Mrs. Bartley raised her eyebrows as she said to the strangers: "This is my daughter, Jean. You must excuse her want of manners."

"You're Mr. Rowlandson, aren't you?" Jean said to the man. "Stephanie has had an accident. She has hurt her ankle——"

"What!" He jumped to his feet while his wife looked up in alarm. "Where is she? Tell me quickly!"

"She's in the woods. I'll show you the place. Mummie, has Daddy not come home? I'll have

to go on to the station when I've taken Mr. Rowlandson to Stephanie."

"Daddy must have been delayed. I'll take you," her mother said at once. "You go with Mr. Rowlandson to the woods and I'll get your case and follow in the car. You can't miss your train."

"Eh? What train? But you can tell me on the way," said Mr. Rowlandson as he hurried Jean out to the car. While they drove down the road she told her companion just why it was so important that she go up to town that evening. She found him very understanding.

"You're sure that your mother can get you to the station in time?" he asked.

Jean nodded. "Quite sure. As soon as we reach Stephanie I'll tear back to Mummie."

As they left the big car at the entrance to the woods she could see the lights of the Morris approaching. Good for Mummie, thought Jean. But there would be no chance of saying goodbye to Daddy. That was the worst of being a doctor. One was never sure of being able to keep appointments.

"Stephanie hated being left by herself," she said to Mr. Rowlandson as they plunged into the gloom of the wood, making their way by the light of the electric torch that the latter carried. "She was terrified of the dark. But I couldn't do anything else."

"Of course not. Poor little wretch, she's as nervous as a cat!" commented her father. "Well, this will teach her not to go wandering off on her own in the future. Ugh! What a night!" He shivered and turned up the collar of his coat. "If she doesn't get a bad cold out of this I'll be surprised—what's the matter?"

Jean had stopped with a cry. They had reached the fallen tree trunk, but there was no sign of Stephanie. "She's gone! I left her here."

"Quite sure that this is the place?" asked Mr. Rowlandson sharply.

"Yes, I know it well. Oh, whatever can she have done!"

"If she's lost herself in this darkness——"

"But she couldn't walk a yard!" protested Jean.

"Then someone found her. She is probably safe at home by now." But Mr. Rowlandson's tone was anxious as he peered into the surrounding dimness. "You don't think she could possibly have left the wood by herself?"

"I'm sure she couldn't. Why, she could hardly stand." Jean saw Mr. Rowlandson's glance at the turbulent river and her face paled. "You don't think——"

"I don't think anything," was his brusque reply, "except that there is nothing to be gained by staying here. We'd better go back to your house and ring up the Grange."

When they joined Mrs. Bartley on the road he explained the situation and she said at once: "Go back to Lyndon. I'll follow you as soon as I've left Jean at the train. Jump in, Jean; there isn't much time."

Jean got into the car, but she shook her head. "I can't go until we find Stephanie. You know I can't, Mummie."

"I understand," said her mother. "But—you realise, Jean, that it means giving up your chance of the Shield?"

"I know," said Jean. And they drove home in silence.

When they went into the hall of Lyndon Mr. Rowlandson was putting down the telephone. "She hasn't gone home." He stared blankly at the strained faces round him.

"Surely anyone who found her would take her home at once," his wife said.

"Or else bring her here," said Jean. "It's nearer, and she knew her mother was coming here."

Just then the clock in the hall struck and Mr. Rowlandson looked over at Jean. "Haven't you a train to catch, young woman?"

"I'm not going," Jean told him, "until we've found Stephanie. I feel that it's my fault that she's lost. Perhaps if I hadn't left her——"

"Don't be foolish, child. You're not to blame." He made no further reference, however, to her going away but paced restlessly up and down

the hall. "I think I'll take the car down to the woods again. We might meet someone who had seen her. Will you come with me, Jean?"

"If only my husband were here he would know what best to do," sighed Mrs. Bartley. "What a night to be out! Jean dear, put on your heavy coat instead of that waterproof. I think the rain is nearly over, but it's getting very cold."

The rain indeed had practically ceased, but the wind was stronger than ever and when the front door was opened a cold blast swept through the house. Mr. Rowlandson was already in the car and Jean was about to follow him when the telephone rang. She was across the hall in a flash.

"Hullo! Hullo!" very faintly she could hear a child's voice. "Is that Lyndon? This is Stephanie Rowlandson. Tell Mummie that I'm——" and the line went dead. At the same instant Jean heard a sharp report like a pistol shot behind her, and, turning, saw through the open door a tree crash down on the avenue.

"It's Stephanie. But I can't hear her any more——" Mr. Rowlandson was beside her now and she handed him the receiver. But there was no sound from it.

"That tree must have fallen across the wire. What bad luck! Another moment and we'd have known where she was. What did she say?"

Jean told him, adding: "We do know that she's all right."

"If only she had had time to say where she was," her father groaned. He looked at his wife. "I can't sit here doing nothing. I'm going out to look for her. Coming, Jean?"

"Yes, I'm coming. If we go down to the police station in the village we could phone the Grange," Jean suggested. "She may have been speaking from there."

Mr. Rowlandson drove as swiftly as he dared along the dark road. They had passed the entrance to the woods and were in sight of the village, when the headlights picked out the ragged figure of a tinker. He carried a pile of jingling pots and pans, and a mongrel dog trailed at his heels.

"We'll stop and ask this fellow if he saw any sign of her," said Mr. Rowlandson.

The tinker looked startled as the big car drew up beside him, but he answered readily: "Yes, sir, I seed a young lady getting into a car a while back. Something wrong with her foot, she had. The gentleman had to carry her."

"Yes, yes? What direction did they take?" asked Mr. Rowlandson as he searched for a coin in his pocket.

The man waved a vague hand down the road he had just traversed. "Went back along that way, they did, sir. Thank you very much, sir."

"Then someone has picked her up all right," said Stephanie's father as they drove on. "But where is she? It's only ten minutes' run to the Grange."

"She's probably there now. Ring them again," Jean urged.

In the village a surprised constable let them use the phone, but could give them no news of the missing child. Nor was there any word of her at the Grange. Mr. Rowlandson's face was very serious as he put down the telephone and proceeded to give the constable a full description of Stephanie.

"No reason to think that she has been kidnapped, have you, sir?" asked the man.

"Not more reason than has any man in my position," was the reply. "There are always people ready to make money that way."

"Oh, no, no!" A cold fear clutched Jean. Why, oh, why had she left Stephanie alone in that wood! "But she rang up——"

"To pass on the terms, perhaps," Mr. Rowlandson said grimly.

In silence they turned the car and drove back to the Bartleys' house. The doctor had not yet come home, but his wife and Mrs. Rowlandson were waiting anxiously for news. One glance at the newcomers' faces told them that there was none.

"You'd better come home, my dear," said Mr. Rowlandson. "We can do no good staying here, and it's getting late."

"I suppose you'll have to go," Mrs. Bartley said regretfully. "At least you'll have the telephone at the Grange, and you know that we will send you word at once if we get news. Your wife looks so tired. She wouldn't take any supper."

With a shock of surprise Jean saw that it was nearly ten o'clock. The wind had dropped a little and as she and her mother went to the front door with the Rowlandsons the moon sailed out from behind the flying clouds. By its light they saw a car come swiftly up the avenue.

"Daddy, at last!" exclaimed Jean and ran forward to meet her father. But for once he paid no heed to her as he got out and lifted a small limp figure from the back seat.

Mrs. Rowlandson gave a horrified cry, but the doctor smiled reassuringly. "It's all right. She's only asleep." With Stephanie in his arms he came into the house, and as he laid the child on the couch in the drawing-room she half woke, murmured something, and then, burying her face in a pillow, went off to sleep again. "Poor youngster, she's worn out!"

"But what happened to her?" demanded Mr. Rowlandson.

"We thought that she was kidnapped," Jean cried.

"We've been so anxious." Mrs. Rowlandson's voice trembled.

The doctor looked at her and said gently: "I'm more than sorry about this. I knew that you would be terribly worried about Stephanie, and I could do nothing to save you that worry."

And then he told them how, driving home that evening, he heard a child crying as he passed the woods. "She was nearly hysterical with fear and pain when I got to her. She told me who she was and I took her to my car intending to drive her straight back to the Grange. I hadn't gone a hundred yards when I was stopped by a boy who had come from a village three miles away to fetch me. His mother had been taken suddenly ill and I was wanted at once. I knew the family well—the woman had been my patient several times—and I knew that they would not have sent for me without due cause. Had I gone on to the Grange with Stephanie it would have meant delay, and delay in this case might prove fatal. So I decided to go straight to the village and telephone you from there. Stephanie told me that her mother was spending the afternoon here." He paused and added quietly: "Well, I got to my patient just in time. Had I waited it would have been too late."

"Then I'm very glad you didn't," exclaimed Mrs. Rowlandson warmly.

"But the telephone?" put in Jean. "Stephanie rang up——"

"Yes, I was too busy with my patient to do it myself. But it seems that the line went dead. The poor child was upset about that."

"The elm on the avenue fell across the wire," Mrs. Bartley explained.

"I see. That was bad luck. Well, they gave her tea, and I fixed up her ankle, and she went off to sleep quite happily." The doctor leant back in his chair. He had had a hard day's work followed by a strenuous evening, and he was very tired. "Sorry about the train, old lady!" he said with a rueful smile at Jean. "I couldn't get here."

"I was going to take her," interposed his wife, "but she wouldn't go."

"I couldn't go, Daddy, till we found Stephanie. I—I hope they'll understand at school. They were so keen about it."

Mr. Rowlandson had gone out to the car to get a rug in which to wrap Stephanie, and as he came in again he heard Jean's words. "Want to try for that Shield, do you?" he asked in his abrupt way.

"I did. But it isn't very important, not as important as looking after ill people," Jean answered as cheerfully as she could. Now that the strain of the evening was over and Stephanie was safe and sound she was beginning to wonder rather dismally what they would say at St. Damian's about her failure to try for the Shield. The Head would understand, of course, but the girls . . .

"Hm!" Mr. Rowlandson was frowning. "Game for an all-night run?" he asked suddenly. "I'll drive you up."

"To town? Tonight!"

"Why not? You can cover up well and go to sleep. Comfortable car. Get you there in plenty of time. What do you say?"

"Say? Why, I think it's a marvellous idea!" Jean's eyes were sparkling. "But—can you really take me?"

"Certainly. Start any time, provided your father will drive my wife and Stephanie home."

"I'll look after them," promised Dr. Bartley. "It's really very good of you, Rowlandson."

"You're not starting off on that long drive without a square meal," said Mrs. Bartley firmly. So while the doctor drove Stephanie and her mother home to the Grange, Jean and Mr. Rowlandson sat down to a substantial supper. When it was over they set off. The big car raced onward through a silent countryside in which every tree and hill-top stood out against a moonlit sky. Jean, too thrilled by this new experience to sleep soundly, dozed in the back of the car. Once she woke up to see the moonlight growing faint, and a thin line of light in the east that showed that dawn was on the way. The next time she woke the sky was a glory of pink and gold as the sun rose on a perfect morning. Mr. Rowlandson drew up at a riverside hotel some miles from town and suggested that they stop and breakfast there. Stiff and cold, Jean climbed from the car, but after a delicious wash in very hot water and a breakfast that tasted better than any she had ever had she felt a different person.

"How does the brain feel? Lively?" inquired Mr. Rowlandson an hour later as he put her down outside the hall where the competition was to be held.

"I don't know," she answered truthfully. "It all depends on the subject of the essay. But anyhow I'm frightfully grateful to you for bringing me here."

Mr. Rowlandson grunted. "Least I could do—after last night," and he drove off before she could say any more.

Jean entered the hall with some misgivings. It was wonderful to have got here, but it wasn't going to be easy to concentrate, with the events of the past eighteen hours running through her mind. If the subject of the essay should be something very dry . . . Last year it had been "The progress of democracy in the twentieth century", and the year before, "The characters of King Lear as revealed by their words". She opened her paper and stared at the single line of print. "Write a short story of two thousand words entitled 'An adventure'."

An adventure! Jean drew a deep breath, picked up her pen, and began to write. . . .

. . . . . .

"But that's all about you and me!" said Stephanie when, during the Christmas holidays, she read the essay that had gained St. Damian's the Shield. "At least I'm in it and so are you, but you've made me much braver than I really was. Why did you do that, Jean?"

Jean laughed. "Well, as you provided me with the material for my story I thought I'd better make you a real heroine."

"And real heroines are always brave. I see." Stephanie's voice was thoughtful. "But I think I'd like to be a real heroine all the time, not just in a story."

"Why not?" agreed Jean. "But if you're thinking of taking another stroll in the woods after dark to test your courage—I wouldn't!"

# Anne of the Running-R

## By ARTHUR GROOM

"HOW'S that, Miss Anne?"

Little bow-legged, leather-skinned Runty Black of the Running-R ranch gave the girths of the pony a final wrench and then went to the creature's head.

"He—he looks all right, Runty," murmured the girl, as she took a firmer grip on her quirt, tugged at the top of her fringed gauntlets and prepared to mount the eighth pony she had tried since her arrival at her uncle's Arizona ranch some six months before. "Wish me luck, will you?"

"Sure!" The little man beamed, his face practically splitting in two with the width of his smile. "Reckon y'll be O.K. now, Miss Anne. Just take it easy for a bit and then give him his head. I guess Rollo rides a sight easier when he's got some of the devil out of his legs. Up you git, Miss Anne! You ain't goin' to let no hoss lick ya, huh?"

Anne Ferris set her lips, put a foot in a stirrup and, a moment later, was in the saddle. She patted the pony's neck and talked softly to him as the little horse-wrangler stepped back, and, shading his eyes against the glare of the noonday sun, watched his pupil with a slightly anxious expression. Ever since the owner of the Running-R had given him the task of looking after Anne Ferris, fresh from England and used only to mounts which even the merest novice could have ridden, he had striven hard to teach his young pupil the ways of the West, so far as horsemanship was concerned.

"O.K!" he yelled. "Let him go!"

64

With a little prayer on her lips, Anne just touched the pony's flanks with her heels and cantered through the paddock gates and on to the rolling range beyond. Rollo skipped about a little, but the girl kept a tight hold on the reins, striving to remember everything that Runty Black had told her.

It was all so different to riding at home, and, to tell the strict truth, she was beginning to think of herself as a failure. If the animal under her proved as hard to ride as the other seven ponies she had tried, then it looked as if she would never achieve her ambition to take part in a beef round-up, not as a passenger in the chuck-waggon or in a buggy, but astride her own mount.

"Be quiet, Rollo!" she hissed at the creature. "What's the matter with you? Oh, durn!" She let go the exclamation as she saw a number of horsemen approaching at full speed across the sun-baked range. The one thing she did not want at that moment was to encounter any of the high-spirited, if kindly, cowhands of the Running-R, and yet here were a whole bunch of them, already chi-hicking as they thundered down upon her.

The girl's mount reared, but, somehow, she managed to retain her seat and then, pulling up the pony, waited anxiously for the cowboys to reach her.

"Howdy, Miss Anne?" greeted a yellow-haired man with the brightest of blue eyes and a missing tooth that gave him a queer, lopsided appearance. "Reckon you've gotten a hoss you kin manage, huh?"

The girl nodded.

"We're sure glad y'r suited, missy!" put in a man who might have been the twin brother of Runty Black. "There ain't nothin' so bad as hoss-trouble. Reckon y'll be settin' out with us on the round-up next week, eh?"

Again Anne nodded. She was a horsewoman enough to know that her mount was getting restless and was hoping wildly that the men would leave her alone to calm the pony. Suddenly the worst happened. Slim

I-B-G—E

Leggard's chestnut, notoriously unreliable, seemed to spin round like a top.

"Heck!" yipped out Bob Leather, he of the missing tooth, as he forestalled the chestnut's vicious attack on the girl's pony. His quirt whistled through the air as he slashed at Rollo's rump. With a startled squeal the creature bounded forward, just in time to avoid having the chestnut's teeth buried in his neck, and a moment later was away like the wind, hoofs thundering over the hard ground and Anne, her whip gone, fighting desperately to keep her precarious seat.

"Goldurn it!" roared Bob Leather. "We'd best git after her."

"No!" A grey-haired man, the strawboss of the Running-R, held up a gloved hand. "Reckon she's O.K., boys; best let her go. If we go on dry-nursing Miss Anne I figure she ain't likely to be a powerful lot of good around the Running-R." The speaker shaded his eyes and nodded approvingly. "Yep!" he drawled. "She's doing swell, fellers! Let's get going!" And, tugging at his reins, he led the cavalcade towards the distant ranch. Only Slim Leggard, whose chestnut had been the cause of all the trouble, delayed long enough to make quite certain that Anne Ferris was still in the saddle and, so far as he could make out, in no danger.

"She's got a good deal of her poor dad in her," he bawled to Bob, when he finally caught up with the others. "I remember the last time John Ferris came out to visit the boss. They were riding——"

"Tell us some other time, Slim!" called back Bob. "If that ain't Chung-Foo lettin' go on that triangle of his, then I ain't never tasted one of his stews. Reckon Miss Anne's ridin' over to the Boxed-Diamond outfit and that means she won't be chi-hicking us all the durned time 'bout not mopping up gravy with our bread. Y' know, fellers," he finished with a laugh, "if Miss Anne gits to comin' on the round-up it'll be more like a Sunday-school picnic than anything else."

So the cowhands put spurs to their mounts and were soon tumbling into the bunkhouse for the midday meal, happy in the thought that the boss's niece would not be there to watch their table-manners with critical eyes as keen as those with which they watched her riding-lessons under Runty Black.

Meanwhile Anne was happier than she had been for weeks and weeks. For the first two or three minutes, after that slash at the pony had sent him bounding forward, it had been touch and go. Rollo had done his best to get rid of his rider, imitating a leaping frog and giving a display of bad-temper that would have brought cheers from a crowd at a Rodeo, but the girl had clung like a leech to the saddle-horn, throwing dignity to the winds in order to keep her seat.

Now, however, it seemed that she had won the fight that had been waged out there on the open range and soon she contrived to get the animal down to an easy lope that covered the ground at an astonishing speed.

"O.K., feller!" she cried with a gay laugh. "Now how about a gallop? As Runty said, we'll really get the devil out of those legs of yours." Even as she spoke Anne shook the reins, dug the heels of her tight-fitting riding-boots into the pony's flanks and gave him his head.

For about a mile the creature thudded along at full stretch, but, quite suddenly, the girl knew that she had failed again. Instinct warned her that Rollo had taken the bit between his teeth and that he was the master of the situation.

"Hold up!" she yelled desperately. "Whoaaaa!" She sawed at the brute's mouth, but all to no purpose—the pony's speed did not slacken in the slightest, and all at once Anne Ferris was aware that the ground was littered with stones.

"Killing Gulch!" she managed to gasp as she saw the mouth of a narrow ravine looming up ahead. For a moment she actually considered leaping from the pony's back and taking her chance, and she had indeed kicked herself free of the wooden stirrups when the creature she rode dashed between two large boulders and put a forefoot into a gopher hole. It was fortunate for Anne that her feet were free; if they hadn't been nothing could have saved her. As it was, she managed to let herself go limp as she was shot, like a stone from a catapult, out of the saddle.

*Crash!*

She hit the ground with a shrill cry of pain, turned a complete somersault, slumped sideways and then was still—very, very still.

Rollo was up again in a matter of seconds. He shook himself, neighed shrilly and then, with a defiant toss of the head, cantered off through Killing Gulch, the tiny stones being scattered in all directions under his flying hoofs.

.    .    .    .    .    .

Anne Ferris groaned as she opened her eyes, only to close them again as the sun glared down on her. Slowly memory came back to her and she groaned again as she opened her eyes once more and realised that her pony was nowhere in sight.

"Keep calm, Anne!" she told herself. "First, any bones broken?" Gingerly she wriggled to a sitting position and gently moved her limbs. No! Nothing seemed to be broken, but her head ached abominably and she knew that things were quite serious. Without food or water it was no joke to be without a mount even ten miles from home. It was unlikely, knowing that she was bound for the Boxed-Diamond Ranch, that anyone would go out from the Running-R to look for her.

"The boys might get anxious," she mused, struggling painfully until she had managed to get her back against a flattish boulder. "Yes, and Runty Black may be coming this way. Don't get panicky, Anne; keep calm. At a pinch I can walk." She gave a shaky laugh as she made the last remark. It *would* be at a pinch with a vengeance, because, like everyone on the range, she wore the riding-boots most suitable for the long, wooden stirrups, the heels high and sloping forward to allow the feet to get a better grip.

"Gosh!" she muttered. "What a mess!"

It was at that moment that she heard the sound so dreaded by those who know the western states of America, the peculiar dry-bone-like rattle made by that killer of the range—the rattlesnake. Anne stiffened and her eyes were staring with fear as she saw the reptile, quite close, poised to strike. Her hand moved to choose a sharp stone to make a desperate bid for life, but, even as her fingers closed over it, there was the crack of a rifle and the snake seemed to leap into the air, twist madly for a second or two and then fall in limp folds to the ground.

The girl's breath was released with a hiss of sheer relief and her eyes shone with gratitude as she looked in the direction from which the shot had come. Then those grey eyes of hers widened as she saw that her rescuer was a loose-limbed, not unhandsome Indian youth of about sixteen years of age, as far as it is possible to judge the age of an Indian. He led a piebald pony towards the girl and halted a matter of ten paces from where she was striving to rise to her feet.

"Give me a hand!" she said.

The Indian boy hauled her upright. "You not hurt, missy?" he asked.

"No!" Anne noted the tribal mark on the young man's cheek, the single scarlet feather in his hair, the clean but patched pants and the loose tunic-like blue shirt that had a beautifully sewn bead belt round it. "Thanks to you. That was a marvellous shot. I say," she went on, her other troubles crowding in upon her, "have you seen a saddled horse? I——" She felt herself blushing. "I was thrown!" she finished.

"So!" The Indian boy nodded solemnly. "Many from England are thrown when they come to Arizona. It is not a disgrace to be thrown. One day you will ride very good."

"But how——?" began the amazed girl. "Who are you?"

"I Little Turtle." The Indian bowed from the waist, stiffly and with old-fashioned courtesy. "I come from Indian Reservation. South!" He pointed. "My father Chief Keen Knife. He own much cattle." Suddenly he frowned and his gaze was direct as he looked at Anne. "But you speak of a horse. I, too, lost a pony, a very lovely pony. I was looking for her when I see rattler——" He stirred the dead snake with a foot in a home-made shoe of some soft leather. "I dismount and kill. I am a good shot with the rifle. Mister Ferris give me rifle." His hand, holding a Winchester repeater, was lifted an inch or so.

Anne looked her surprise. "You know my uncle—the owner of the Running-R?"

The Indian shook his head and nodded at the same time.

"I know him—yes," said Little Turtle. "But Mister Bob Ferris did not give me rifle. That given by Mister John Ferris when he come from England. He was your father!" The last was a simple plain statement of fact uttered with all the calmness of the American Indian. "I know you are Miss Ferris. I see you ride many time. You like my sister. Her name White Cloud."

Anne sat down. She had suddenly remembered her father telling her about this Indian boy he had befriended, and the thought of her father, whose death was still so fresh in her mind, made her want to blubber aloud—and that would never, never do. She strove to pull herself together.

"Yes," she said. "He was my father. He spoke about you. Is your sister with you?" She shaded her eyes.

Sadness filled the boy's dark eyes. "She die when sickness come to Reservation. Last winter."

"Oh, I'm so sorry!"

"You sorry for me," said Little Turtle. "I sorry for you." He smiled gently. "You also lose pony and me lose pony, too. You are thirsty?" The last remark was accompanied by a movement as the speaker detached a water-bottle from the beautifully fashioned saddle of the piebald pony, and then, uncorking it, held it out to Anne.

The girl drank gratefully and she had just returned the water-bottle when she became aware of a tenseness in the Indian's attitude.

"What——?" she began and whirled about. Then her breath came in a low whistle of sheer admiration as she saw an animal picking its way delicately through the scattered stones and boulders of the gulch. It was the loveliest creature she had ever seen and, instinctively, she took a step forward.

"No! You leave her." The words were commanding and strong fingers bit into the flesh of the girl's arm. "Only my little sister and I, Little Turtle, go near the pony. Once"—the voice was low but very clear —"she nearly kill a bad man who try to steal from White Cloud. You understand?"

What made Anne Ferris act the way she did she could never explain, not even to her own satisfaction, but perhaps it had something to do with her repeated failures to stay for long in the saddle of any of the mounts that had been found for her by Runty Black and her uncle and guardian. Anyway, she was quicker even than Little Turtle as she whirled round and, wrenching her arm free, strode forward straight for the oncoming pony.

"*No!*" The Indian boy's voice rose shrilly. "*No! She will kill you. Come back!*"

The creature had halted and its eyes rolled wildly in its head as its nostrils flared to show the red veins like scarlet threads running through the soft skin. A sense of caution that she had inherited with her spirit from her father warned her to obey the command of the Indian boy, but sheer devilment, or rather an urge to prove that she was a good horse-woman and was not afraid of anything that stood on four legs, banished caution.

With right hand outstretched she went slowly forward towards the motionless pony, even as the boy spoke to the animal.

"She not hurt you, Flower," he called clearly. "She is a friend. A friend."

The creature danced sideways for a moment or two and then was still again.

"Aaaah!" Anne let go her breath as she put a hand on to the pony's bridle. Then the unbelievable happened, something that Little Turtle still talks about and is likely to talk about all his life. The lovely creature bent her head and nuzzled the girl, butting her gently and uttering a soft little half-whimpering and half-whinnying sound as her right front foot pawed the ground so delicately that the dust was hardly disturbed.

"Missy!" There was amazement, joy and happy laughter in Little Turtle's voice as he came forward. He had carefully ground-hitched the piebald, Indian fashion, so both hands were free to be held out for Anne Ferris to take. "I clasp your hands, missy," he cried. "See! As will my father—Keen Knife!" He had imprisoned the girl's palms as she let go the pony to accept his greeting, but the animal did not move. "Flower belongs to you now," went on the boy. "I—no, White Cloud, my sister give her to you. Yes, that must be so. It must be!" He let go the girl's hand and fondled the pony's soft, almost silken muzzle. "You like that Missy Anne own you, Flower?"

Again there came that half-whimper and half-whinny from the animal.

"We go!" said Little Turtle, turning to Anne. "I ride with you—yes?"

The girl just stared at him. "But I cannot accept such a gift," she cried. "My uncle will buy the pony."

Anger smouldered in the Indian boy's dark eyes and he drew himself up to his full height and stood with folded arms, appearing to be inches taller than his companion.

"No!" he said sternly. "I take Flower to Lawson City to sell, but when trader offer much money, many dollars, I tell him that I change my mind. That is why I return today with the pony. But now all is changed. The Spirit of White Cloud would not let me sell and then she send you to be saved from the snake. The Great Spirit speak to Little Turtle." A note of pleading came into the speaker's voice. "So you talk no more of giving money for my sister's pony?"

Anne looked into those dark eyes and nodded. "I speak no more of money!" she said.

Five minutes later the two were riding back towards the Running-R ranch. The girl had decided that she would be too late to go on to the Boxed-Diamond outfit and, indeed, was anxious to show her uncle and, in particular, the cowhands her mastery over the pony. Her heart sang with happiness all the way, because for the first time in her life she was perfectly at home in the saddle and, because of that, the range seemed to wear a more friendly look. It was as if she was seeing it, in all its beauty, for the very first time.

"Yippppeeee! Hi-ti-*hiiiii*!"

It was hard to believe that that shrill cry came from Anne Ferris's lips, but it did and it brought little Runty Black, Bob Leather and three or four other men hurrying towards the riders. Anne swerved her mount, her heels drumming against the creature's flanks, and then, tugging at the reins, rode full-tilt towards the paddock gate. Someone ran to open it but was a great deal too late. Like a bird the pony sailed over the obstacle and the rider twisted in the saddle as she jumped to laugh at the stupefied looks on the faces of the men.

"Anne!"

A bull-like roar made the girl turn as she slid from the saddle.

"What does this mean?" demanded the boss of the Running-R. "Whose pony is that?"

"Mine!" the girl faced her uncle and the story poured from her lips. "You will let me keep her, Uncle," she begged. "I am sure Keen Knife would approve; and, Uncle, now I can go with you on the round-up. I can, can't I?"

The rancher dived a hand into a pocket of his blue jeans and advanced towards the pony with a piece of apple on his palm. He was still several paces away when Flower reared, her hoofs poised perilously over the man's head.

In a flash, a slight, agile figure in a pair of light-coloured pants and a shirt had leapt between Robert Ferris and the pony.

"Please," said Little Turtle. "She kill you, maybe! Only Little Turtle, my sister White Cloud and Missy Anne safe with Flower."

The rancher held the piece of apple out to his niece.

"I reckon he's right, Anne," he said. "Here, you'd better give your pony her tit-bit."

The girl's shrill cry of delight rang high and clear. "Then I may keep her?" she cried.

"Heck!" grunted Runty Black from behind her. "I figure you'd have a goldurned job to get rid of that pony, Miss Anne! I guess you were just made for each other."

# JESSICA'S MUSEUM
### By BETTY E. SPENCE

"**W**HY didn't you count ten before you spoke?" asked Betsy bitingly.

"Or not spoken at all," added Lulu no less scathingly.

Jessica looked beseechingly at the fourth member of the small coterie, hoping for some soothing gesture, but sweet, plump, loyal Catherine only shook her head despairingly, as if to say, "Well, what could you expect?"—and this hurt the most of all.

Jessica thrust out her stubborn chin just a little bit more, tightened her lips in case they gave away their tell-tale quivering, and looked her accusers squarely in the eye.

"Why didn't *you* think of an idea," she countered in return. "You just sat there like a lot of sheep looking at me to make the first suggestion. Now you don't like it, and I—oh, I don't care!" Too near tears now to argue further, Jessica turned sharply on her heel and hurried on alone.

But in spite of this show of bravado she was feeling as uncertain and wretched over her "clever" idea as they were.

It had all started so innocently that morning with Miss Penston—Penny to the girls of her friendly, enterprising, little private school—calling them into the front parlour of the one-time farmhouse. The girls, packed tighter than any sardines, rustled, and coughed, and twittered, and wondered what their headmistress had in store for them. She did not keep them long in doubt.

"I don't have to tell you girls," she said, "the predicament this school has found itself in since the old barn was burnt down. As a barn it made us a very good hall where you older girls will remember we have put on a succession of concerts and prize-givings, and even drill displays when the weather was unfavourable. It was our gymnasium and our lecture-room; even when this school was a farmhouse, the barn was not put to a better use. Three months ago we lost it for ever, and, you must all agree, it has left a gap in our school-life both literally and figuratively speaking." She broke off here to scan them all with her shrewd blue-grey eyes and observe their reactions. They all wore a set, melancholy look as if she were dwelling on the passing of an old and honoured friend. "Now as you know, it is our annual sport's day in a fortnight's time, and, as usual, Mrs. Pakenham is lending us her marquees and tents, and other valuable assistance. And it was she who suggested a way in which we might be able to build a new school-hall on the ashes of the old. We could combine a fête with our sport's display, and charge a small admission fee. Then you girls will be in charge of the side-shows. I would like you to make some suggestions. Now, don't all jabber at once. I want you to think this over very carefully, and not just shout out the first idea that comes into your head. For instance, a coconut-shy—as one of you shouted—would be too unprofitable as the expenditure on stock would be more than it's likely to bring in."

"Unless we nail them down like they do at real fêtes," interrupted someone, *sotto voce*.

Miss Penston heard and smiled.

"That has yet to be proved, and it is neither a very original idea nor an honest one. Come along, girls; let's have some really worthwhile suggestions."

"A bring-and-buy stall."

"A white-elephant stall."

"Raffles."

"Guessing one's weight."

"Hoop-la."

"Treasure hunt."

"A handicrafts stall."

Miss Penston held up her hand, and the suggestions died out.

"Well, girls, I do know now that you've been constant visitors to village fêtes and church bazaars—but has no one a really original suggestion to make?"

It was at that fateful moment that Jessica felt the IDEA being born within her and struggling to give life. Catching the eyes of her three closest friends, and encouraged by their looks, for her end-of-term reports nearly always emphasised on her originality, not always complimentarily, but sufficiently for her to have earned the title of the most original girl in the school, she wagged her arm expectantly and answered to Miss Penston's look of enquiry:

"Please, Miss Penston—*a museum!*"

"Yes?" Miss Penston encouraged her.

"I thought that if I could have one of the smaller tents and collect some interesting exhibits and have them on view, and then charge admission—it might be quite a success. I've got a piece of Roman pottery that my uncle dug up in his orchard—and—and I'm sure I could get together a lot of other things, too."

"There would have to be a great many other things, Jessica, to attract an attendance. But I must say it sounds very hopeful and the most original idea we've had yet. Well, girls, think it over among yourselves. We can't spend any further time discussing it now, as the bell will be going shortly."

Jessica and her friends sauntered out of the room, well aware of the impression they had made, and walking on air in consequence. It might have been Jessica's idea in the first place, but it quite definitely belonged to all of them now, for, like the Three Musketeers, their motto was "One for all and all for one". That is until Betsy burst their bubble of satisfaction by enquiring, on their homeward journey:

"What else have you got to put in the museum besides that bit of Roman pottery, Jessica?"

Jessica stopped dead. Her eyes grew large and wondering, and her cheeks pink with embarrassment.

"Why—eh—I haven't really thought yet. Oh, but I expect I'll soon get a few things together."

It was the turn of the others to stop short and look surprised, and their faces went red with anger.

"*Jessica Mason!* Do you mean to say that all you've got is that piece of Roman pottery?"

"It's a very interesting exhibit," retorted Jessica, on the defensive at once.

"You mean it *was*. Everybody in the school has seen it at least twice, and goodness knows how many times it's turned up at Sunday-school bazaars and the Young People's Guild displays. I reckon everybody in Dibsdale knows that piece of Roman pottery by heart!"

"What have you got to put in the museum, then? I notice you soon took the limelight for my idea. Now help me out with it!"

They saw the fairness of this and came forward with the offer of, provisionally, Lulu's young brother's collection of bird's eggs; Betsy's bottle of coloured sand from the Isle of Wight; and a velvet pincushion in the shape of a heart embroidered by Catherine's great-grandmother.

"But that's only four things, and we must at least have fifty," wailed Betsy. "Oo-oh, we'll be the laughing stock of the school, and did you see the glares Robina Jackson and Shirley Davies gave us when Miss Penston singled you out for praise? They'll never let us live it down. And all because you were too quick with your ideas—Miss Clever Jessica."

After that they had all said things they did not mean, and Jessica, walking on alone, began to feel misunderstood and misunderstanding in turn. She was soon joined by Catherine, who slipped a warm, friendly hand into her own.

"Don't take any notice of them," she said comfortingly. "They're only disappointed because they think the museum is a scrummy idea, and now they're frightened in case we might not be able to carry it out. They don't realise that half the fun will be getting the contents together."

"You are such a comfort, Cath," rejoined Jessica gratefully, squeezing her hand in return. "But Betsy is right. I have been too clever this time. I haven't a single object in mind except those we have already mentioned —and only two weeks until Sports Day, too."

"Don't worry. To start off we'll try our own families. There's sure to be lots of old stuff tucked away in corner cupboards and forgotten about. I've got one old aunt who could furnish an antique shop with the exhibits on her mantelpiece at least!"

They laughed together and felt more hopeful. Betsy and Lulu, who had been loitering a little ashamedly behind, came hurrying up and asked to be let into the joke.

"We'll never find anything of interest in *this place*," Betsy retorted despondently, familiarity cloaking the fact that tourists from all over the world bore down on this corner of the Midlands to gloat over the country lanes and shady, wooded walks where Shakespeare may have roamed as a youth.

Since babies, the four girls had been living among surroundings that had hardly changed since Queen Elizabeth's time, and they took for granted the black-and-white half-timbered houses with shaggy roofs tumbling about twinkling latticed windows set high in gables, that visitors stopped to exclaim over.

Their perfect jewel of a village was set in a peaceful backwater of meadows and woods and gently sloping hills, caused by the powerful by-pass that tore its way more deeply into Warwickshire on its race to the north, and left them in a quiet unchanging void, rarely stirred by the world outside. Within cycling distance was the lovely Forest of Arden, and once Miss Penston had taken the senior girls there to act *As You Like It* in its original setting.

"You'd think," said Jessica to herself, as later that day she looked out from her bedroom window across the valley to the summer meadows rising gently to the woods behind, "that in the midst of all this—this *past*, I'd find something for my *museum*!"

At the end of that week they had just over a dozen exhibits in hand. Two of these, a thick white mug with a picture of King George V's coronation on it, and a short squat vase with "A Present from Brighton" splashed across it, could not, in the strict sense of the word, be called museum pieces, but, for the want of anything more appropriate, were being included with more legitimate things. As Lulu so aptly put it: "We're not in a position to be choosy!"

On the whole, their relatives had rallied around them very well. They had produced: (i) an elaborately carved Ostrich's egg, and a stuffed vulture (from Lulu's uncle who was a retired ship's steward); (ii) a Victorian backboard belonging to an old friend of Betsy's great-aunt, who had actually worn it as a girl—this undoubtedly increasing its historic value—and they intended to see that it was duly labelled with this information; (iii) a George II silver salt-spoon; (iv) a sampler that had been in Catherine's family longer than her own great-grandmother; (v) a newspaper printed on the day Queen Victoria died and so wafer thin that the girls held their breaths every time they were forced to handle it; and (vi) a pair of baby shoes belonging to a man who if he had lived would have been over a hundred. All these they considered to be genuine museum pieces, but they had half a dozen others that came in the doubtful category, such as a wedding dress belonging to one of Jessica's aunts, and so frilly and short, that Jessica felt like a little girl going off to her first party when she tried it on. This aunt's husband had also offered her his spare set of false-teeth which, he said, he had always suspected should be in a museum, but Jessica, intercepting the look his wife gave him, refused with such a look of cold dignity that she hoped it would make him realise that the inhabitants of Dibsdale would pay threepence to see something better than his old teeth!

But still, they had not anything like as many exhibits as they needed, and the days were running out quickly.

"There's only one thing to be done," said Jessica with resignation. "We'll just have to canvass. We can promise those who lend us anything towards the museum to view it afterwards at half-price. That's sure to do the trick."

There were only two roads in Dibsdale. The village road that ran in a loop from the by-pass, and on which the church and the inn and the older houses were situated, and a smaller, unmade road on both sides of which were scattered the newer type houses. This meandered out into open country past farms and farm cottages and eventually leading to Dibsdale Hall.

To think of Dibsdale without the Hall was to think of a fire without smoke, and yet, to most of the inhabitants the Hall was just a stack of chimney's behind a high brick wall, coloured and made intriguing by the rumours that fed on it.

Old Miss Marlowe lived there, the last of the Marlowes to have lived there since Shakespeare's time, and twice a year, on Easter Sunday and Christmas Day, she emerged from her fastness and attended church. This was the only time the villages set eyes on her, and the old grey stone church was crowded beyond its capacity on those days. Rumours had it that she was as poor as a church mouse and as proud as a peacock; that she lived in one room to save expenses and that she and her equally as aged servant were dying a slow death from starvation; that apart from Mr. Pakenham the vicar, she had not spoken to anybody for ten years! But the rumour that heightened the interest in her by the younger set was that years ago she had been a lovely girl, the belle of all the hunt balls in the county, that it had been a sight to see her going all dressed up in her carriage to pay calls on the other big houses around. But, funnily enough, nobody seemed to remember when the metamorphosis from young lovely girl to withered old lady in dusty black had taken place, so that even the oldest member of the village found it hard to connect the two, and in the minds of every one there were two Miss Marlowes—the young one who belonged to the past, and the old one who belonged to the present, and there was nothing in between.

Jessica had once met the old one when she had inadvertently stepped in her way when they were both leaving church. She had been aware of a pair of piercing black eyes snapping at her in vexation, and a thin voice that asked her if she knew where she was going. After that she had hoped never to cross her path again.

So that when Betsy took up her suggestion and put it to her and Catherine to take the country road, she remembered that forbidding look and shivered. "I couldn't try Dibsdale Hall, Catherine; I couldn't," she faltered.

"We'll just take the houses in turn," countered Catherine imperturbably.

Of course, they had no luck. Most of the houses they called at were owned by relatives of the four girls, who had already lent all they had, apart from the fact that the majority of them being modern houses had few antiques let alone museum pieces.

"Betsy knew something suggesting this road for us," grumbled Jessica, when they drew blank for the fourteenth time.

"In more ways than one, too," sighed Catherine. It was a hot afternoon, and the sun poured down on them without mercy. They were out in open country now, and the sweet-smelling lime trees that had shaded the road at first were now a long way behind them. Either side of them, the woven hedges, peculiar to the country roads of

Warwickshire, braided the sloping green meadows. Further along, they came to a merry tumbling brook that was fed from the waters of the Avon, and here they stopped to moisten their handkerchiefs and wipe the dust and heat from their faces. They had passed the last of the farms and now there was only Dibsdale Hall, and it was Jessica's turn.

"I may as well get it over with," she said heroically. "You stay down at the gates, Catherine, because if we have to bolt for it I can run faster than you, so I'll give you the advantage."

The heavy wrought-iron gates, backed by iron screens that shut out the view of the drive beyond, groaned rebelliously as the two girls combined their weights, and thrust them open, revealing a tangled over-growth of laurel trees and rhododendron bushes. Above these they could see a large old house standing on a slight rise, with the twisted chimney-stacks of the Tudor period, and the graceful colonnaded façade of the Georgian age.

From the first Marlowe in Elizabeth's time to one during Victoria's reign, each had added a little of the architecture of their own time, but for the past hundred years there had been no alterations and no additions, and now it had a dingy, neglected air in keeping with its lawns and flower-beds that were choked with weeds.

Jessica walked on, feeling a veritable Daniel as she neared the house, which looked, on closer inspection, so much more decayed than it did from the road.

"Well, child—do you know where you're going this time?" asked a voice out of the bushes on her right.

Jessica jumped, looked all about her, and then became aware of a pair of unblinking black eyes peering at her through the purple fronds of a buddleia tree. She felt the words of explanation dry up in her throat. It would have been bad enough to have formed her pleas waiting at the front door, but how much worse was it to be confronted whilst still unprepared!

The old lady came into view. She was wearing a gardening smock over her black dress and an ancient straw hat instead of her customary black bonnet.

She turned and looked down the drive to where Catherine's dark head was bobbing backwards and forwards from behind the half-open gates in unconstrained curiosity.

"Is that the same head appearing each time, or is the rest of your school waiting down there?" she asked dryly.

Jessica's nervousness exploded in a chuckle. Whatever else she had expected from the old lady of the manor, it wasn't a gleam of humour, and now, boldly raising her eyes to meet the black ones, she saw them crinkled in a friendly smile.

"I'm not such a terrifying old woman, am I?" asked Miss Marlowe wistfully. "Though it annoys me exceedingly to see the young ones scatter from my path whenever I *do* go out. One would think I was going to eat them!"

Jessica, who had been guilty of this herself, and felt that this remarkable old lady remembered it, too, began to stutter nervously over her words.

"Please don't think I'm prying," she said. "I've—I've come on a really important errand."

"In that case we must discuss it over tea. It is many years since I had a caller," added Miss Marlowe softly. "Please ask your friend of the bobbing head to join us also."

Jessica ran to fetch Catherine whilst Miss Marlowe slowly made her way up to the house. By the time she had reached the flight of stone steps that led up to the front door, they had caught up with her, both a little flushed at the thought of tea in the house of mystery.

The heavy front door was swinging slightly ajar, and they followed their hostess into a wide spacious hall, cool and dark after the heat and glare outside. The splendour of the white and gilt walls, the cherubims painted on the ceiling, the carving on the massive staircase curving to the upper floor, the glittering of the crystal chandelier overcame the girls with its magnificence. Though the same pall of dirt and neglect hung over here as it did outside, they saw only the grandeur that once had been.

Breaking into their fascinated gazing came a little old lady, even more withered looking than Miss Marlowe, with grey hair pulled back from a bony face, and watery eyes that peered at them closely from behind rimless glasses.

"You didn't tell me you were expecting company," she said frettishly.

"I did not know myself," answered Miss Marlowe, quite unperturbed. "Please serve tea in the drawing-room, Martha."

"The drawing-room!" The old servant could not have been more astounded if she had been ordered to serve it in the bathroom. "But you ain't bin in the drawing-room for twenty years!"

"That is an omission I am rectifying this afternoon," her mistress retorted. "Now hurry, please."

With dignity she led the girls through white, or what were once white, and gilt double doors into a large, rectangular, richly furnished room. The blinds were all down at the windows, and as Miss Marlowe went along sending each one up with a defiant snap the sun came in by degrees, and showed up the dust and cobwebs of years of unuse.

Presently the door opened again, and Martha, looking offended, slammed down a tray on a low table of carved, black wood. The tray held a mixture of old silver and chipped china. There was a plate of roughly cut bread and butter, and three very rocky rock cakes.

Miss Marlowe looked at them ruefully.

"There was a time, my dears, when I served bread and butter cut so thinly it could form into rolls, and sponge fingers that melted at a touch. Entertaining, as far as we old people in this house are concerned, is, I'm afraid, a lost art. However, Martha's tea is always good, so let me give you a cup."

Sipping at the scalding tea, Jessica shyly explained the reason for her visit. She went back a long way and told Miss Marlowe all about the farmhouse school and how Miss Penston had first started it ten years before as an alternative to the little village school and the big county school five miles away. How funds had never been very free, and when the old barn which acted as their school hall was accidentally burnt to the ground, Miss Penston had no means by which to replace it. Miss Marlowe listened in attentive silence, interrupting now and again to mutter: "Dear me, and I didn't know"; or "Miss Penston seems a really admirable person. I would like to meet her."

Catherine said not a word. She sat on the edge of her chair, swinging her legs, choking over her cake, and not taking her fascinated gaze from their hostess. It was a wonderful moment when Miss Marlowe promised to lend them as many objects as they could handle. "Martha and I will pack them this very afternoon, and I'll get George the carrier to deliver them to you," she promised.

"The girls walked off down the drive afterwards wondering if they had not just experienced a wishful dream.

"It just can't be true," Jessica said again and again. "Oh, isn't she a darling! Do you know something, Cath? I don't believe she has been shutting the village *out*—I believe the village has been shutting her *in*. You see, all her own relations and acquaintances have been dying off one by one, leaving her only that funny old servant. She did not know any of the village people very well to start with; they weren't so democratic in her young days, and now she's too old or too proud to try. She must be poor to let that beautiful old house go to decay like that. D'you think we ought to pay her for the hire of her things—that is, if we make enough out of our museum? After all, even a few shillings would be very acceptable to her, no doubt."

They met Betsy and Lulu at the junction of the two roads, and all they had to show for their afternoon's work was a piece of dried twig, which, they had been told, was a cutting from the famous mulberry tree in Shakespeare's garden at Stratford-on-Avon.

"Well, I'm glad you think so," said Jessica, looking at it doubtfully. "But, girls," she added brightly, "just wait until you hear *our* news!"

If they were excited then it was nothing to the excitement that greeted the large wooden crate that George the carrier left at Jessica's house the next day. It was nailed down, and after prising open the lid they came upon a layer of straw.

"My, it has been packed professionally!" exclaimed Betsy. "Every piece in tissue paper, too. Well, here goes, girls—let's see what old junk she's sent."

One by one they unwrapped the articles, and as each was displayed their eyes grew rounder and their tongues more stilled.

There were exquisite pieces of filigree silver; transparent hand-painted china; ivory statuettes; heavy old jewellery starred with glowing precious stones that caught and held all the colours of the rainbows; porcelain figures with crinoline dresses the texture of fine lace; gold and silver snuff-boxes with richly enamelled tops; and even a little leather purse of old golden guineas. It was just as if Flint's treasure had been dumped down in the middle of Jessica's bedroom. The girls sat back on their heels and stared at it in speechless wonder. Jessica was the first to come back to life.

"To think we thought her *poor*," she murmured. "I was even going to offer her a few shillings for the use of these things. Why, they must be worth a fortune! Don't you think we ought to return them. Supposing we lost any or broke one of them."

Betsy jumped on this idea at once.

"For goodness' sake, Jessica—have sense! She must know what they're worth, and yet she's lent them to us, hasn't she? Just think of Robina Jackson and Shirley Davies when they see this lot. They'll turn green with envy!"

So it was that the next afternoon, the little red tent in the corner of the playing field was a hub around which the interest of the fête wheeled. Always there was a queue awaiting admission, and though Jessica admitted to herself that this was due more to a curiosity to see the belongings of the lady of the manor than a wish to be educated by the other museum exhibits, it was gratifying to know that her project was bringing in more money than all the other sideshows put together.

"There's a scrummy-looking individual staring very hard at Miss Marlowe's things," Catherine whispered to her once. "I'm going to keep my eye on him—you never know!"

She did this to such an extent that the "scrummy-looking individual" became quite confused and left. The next they saw of him he was in earnest conversation with Miss Penston, and they wondered if she was demanding to know his intentions. And then who should be the next to purchase an admission ticket but Miss Marlowe herself! As this information filtered around the playing-fields the queue grew to such proportions that it had to snake in and out of the other sideshows, and Betsy ran out of tickets, and had to borrow a roll from the disgruntled stall-holders next door.

The lady of the manor, quite unaware that she was now the chief exhibit, walked slowly around the makeshift stands, admiring the things on display that she had not personally provided.

"Very admirable," she said to Jessica as she passed out again. "I don't think I have enjoyed an afternoon like this for a long, long time. Now your kind headmistress has promised me tea, and after that I shall look forward to the drill display."

It was the best sports day in the memory of the farmhouse school. At the finale, when the girls marched round the field to the strains of the village band and passed the little platform reserved for Miss Penston and her staff and saw Miss Marlowe and the "scrummy-looking individual" sitting up there looking quite at home, they thought something portentous had happened. It was not long before they found out what it was.

The next morning, Jessica was sent for by Miss Penston. She came back to the classroom with sparkling eyes, and flushed cheeks, and so bubbling over with news that the rest of the class could hardly contain themselves until recess to hear what it was.

Then they crowded around Jessica demanding to know the outcome of the interview.

"You'll never believe it," she cried breathlessly. "It's a dream come true! It's a hope realized! It's a *miracle*! You know your 'scrummy-looking individual', Cath? Well, it appears he is a world-famous collector of antiques and other works of art, staying at the inn on a short holiday, incognito. When he saw Miss Marlowe's things yesterday, he immediately contacted her, and what do you think—he offered her a fantastic sum of money for them!"

"And she refused——?"

"She did not! She says the money has no interest for her, but the treasures have less as they clutter up the place and are a great responsibility—so she sold them."

"But if she doesn't want the money——"

"That's the point. She does want it but not for herself. I can't believe this, and you won't at first either, and poor Miss Penston is sitting in her study in a daze frightened to wake up—but Miss Marlowe has given all that money to *us*—*the school*—to use as we like. Either to build a new hall, or build a new school if we like—or—well, she's given us something else, too. She has given us *Dibsdale Hall*."

A profound silence greeted this. It was too much to take in all at once.

"But why?" asked somebody in a subdued voice at length.

"Because, she says, we have the nucleus of a grand little school here, and in a bigger place it could be expanded to benefit not only the village but the country as a whole. Then the estate is so vast that we could have tennis courts, and hockey fields, and even a swimming pool built. She says we wouldn't have to worry about having a school hall built, because there is a great ball-room at the manor that would make a marvellous hall. Oh, she gave hosts of reasons, but I believe that the chief one—and one that she didn't give—is because she is lonely."

The other girls began to laugh then.

"Now you *are* romancing, Jessica. We can believe all the rest, but not that. Just as if anybody in their right minds would change their peaceful home into a school for girls just because they were lonely."

The next afternoon, at Miss Marlowe's request, Jessica went to tea with her again. This time the drawing-room had been dusted, and the table was laid with a beautiful lace cloth, and there were rolls of wafer-thin bread and butter and chocolate biscuits and tiny iced fairy cakes.

"Well, my dear, it's all settled," said Miss Marlowe as she poured tea out of a chaste silver tea-pot that had not been included in the museum exhibits. "Miss Penston has finally agreed to my plans, and the workmen are taking over next week to do the necessary alterations. It will be very satisfying to see this old place come to life again."

"Oh, Miss Marlowe," cried Jessica greatly daring, "we've been so *wrong* about you. We thought you were proud, and stiff, and poor, and all the time you are the friendliest and most generous person there ever was."

"But no, dear, I was proud," answered Miss Marlowe gently. "I was too proud to let people know how lonely I was, and I was proud in a way of my family possessions, letting them beguile me into thinking that they mattered more than people. But they don't, my dear; you proved that when you came that day and awakened my interest in you young people's problems and achievements. Now I have exchanged a few worldly objects for a host of new friends, and I feel richer already. You realize, don't you, that Martha and I come with the school?"

"As if we'd want it without you," cried Jessica sincerely.

"And Miss Penston has even offered me a place on her staff," added Miss Marlowe proudly. "I am going to be in charge of the needlework class——"

"Then I pity the girls," said Martha, coming into the room with some more hot water and overhearing this last remark. "I've known you fifty years, but I've never yet bin able to teach you to do a darn you can't see the other side of the room."

"She's right," sighed Miss Marlowe when Martha had gone. "So perhaps she had better be in charge of the needlework class and Miss Penston must think of something else for me." Then she laughed like a young girl. "Perhaps she'll take me as a pupil with the little ones—I've got so much to learn all over again." Her voice softened, and she stretched out her hand across the table and warmly clasped that of Jessica's. "And it is all due to you, my dear, and your funny little idea of having a 'museum'. Now raise your cup, Jessica, and we will drink a toast. To the success and fame of the Manor House School, and one day, may Jessica Mason be head girl!"

# A DIFFICULT DECISION

*By DORIS M. LEE*

VALERIE BARCLAY looked at the filmy net frock dotted with sequins which lay on her friend Diana Layton's bed. Beside it were silver sandals, nylons of gossamer thinness, a pretty evening bag.

Round the bedroom on hangers were several other pretty frocks, a top coat with suit to match, just right for travelling.

Diana's father was wealthy, and nothing seemed too good for his fifteen-year-old daughter.

"The seats are booked on the plane. In a week's time we shall be off," Diana was saying to Valerie, who could not help feeling that some people had all the luck.

Next minute she could hardly believe her ears, for Diana was asking her to come, too, on this wonderful trip to Paris.

"Cousin Sheila let us down this morning. Her seat was booked, and her room at the hotel. You simply *must* come," said the rather spoiled girl airily.

For a few seconds Valerie could not answer, and, taking silence for consent, Diana's delicate features were alight with pleasure.

"Think of it—dancing, concerts, oh, lashings of fun for a glorious fortnight," she cried, clapping her hands and skipping round the room in delight.

But now Valerie shook her head. "I'd love to, Diana," she said haltingly, "but Mums isn't a bit strong after her operation. With the twins home for the hols, she'll find an awful lot of extra work to do in our old-fashioned house. I can't leave her to cope with everything single-handed."

Diana was used to having her own way. She could not believe anyone would turn down an offer like this! Her red lips pouted as she replied: "But, Valerie, surely you've *some* friend or relation who would come and help your mother while you're away? A chance like this doesn't come every day."

"I know it doesn't," answered Valerie, with another glance at the dainty dance dress, at the smart beach-wear and the many other signs of luxury which Diana took as a matter of course.

"Well," replied that pampered young person loftily, "the offer holds good for a day or two—unless Mummy asks some far off-distant relation to join us. Ugh!" Diana shuddered in horror at this idea, and once more begged Valerie to decide quickly.

The sixteen-year-old looked very thoughtful as she walked homewards. Diana was quite right. Such a chance did not come twice in a lifetime.

"Not to the likes of me," Valerie told herself, "yet, if I do accept, and Mums crocked up again, I'd never forgive myself."

She decided to say nothing about the suggestion for the present, guessing that her mother would insist on her going away with her wealthy school friend.

Valerie found her mother had done a pile of ironing as well as turning out the twins' bedroom in readiness for their arrival from boarding school next day.

"You go and lie down. I'll see to supper tonight," Valerie said firmly, with one glance at Mrs. Barclay's white face. "You should have left the ironing to me," the schoolgirl added.

It was extremely warm in the large old-fashioned kitchen as she set to work preparing macaroni cheese, a treacle tart, and some chocolate cakes which were a special favourite with Peter and Paul.

They were ten years old, jolly lads, but a bit of a handful at times, as Valerie well knew.

She popped her cakes into the oven, thinking how jolly it would be if she were earning money so that they could have more help.

At supper Valerie was very quiet, thinking once again of Diana's luck in having a wealthy father to provide her with expensive clothes, an exciting holiday and everything else the heart of a girl could desire.

"Do you feel all right, dear?" Mrs. Barclay asked. "You look quite pale."

"It was so hot in the kitchen, Mums. Feels like a storm," Valerie replied, and got up to open the window a little wider.

Not a leaf stirred outside; the air felt electric with heat. After supper, when Valerie and her mother sat in the garden, it was no cooler.

"We both need a holiday," Mrs. Barclay remarked as she began on some darning. "I wrote to Mrs. Sims to see if she could have us for a week or ten days, but she is full up to the end of the season."

Valerie smiled a little wearily. "The lads will be disappointed not to go to the farm this year," she said. She now noticed that, besides looking very pale, her mother was also looking very worried.

As if she guessed Valerie's thoughts, Mrs. Barclay looked up and wrinkled her brows in a worried frown. "I can't think why we haven't heard from Uncle Don lately. It's nearly three months since I had his last letter," she said. Uncle Don was Mrs. Barclay's only brother, who lived in America.

"Perhaps there'll be a letter in the morning," said Valerie, and got up restlessly and began to walk round the garden. The air was humid with heat, and now the sky began to darken and thunder could be heard in the distance.

Mrs. Barclay hated storms. She instantly made tracks for the house as lightning flickered ominously between the trees at the end of the garden and soon rain began to fall in earnest.

"No good going to bed while this lasts," said Valerie, when the storm had rattled and roared round the house for over an hour.

"All the same, I'll go up and lie down," said Mrs. Barclay. "I've got a wretched headache."

Valerie still felt extremely restless. She got a book, but could not read, took out her shorthand books and tried to study, but in vain.

At last, however, the thunder died away, the lightning flickered fitfully between the trees, and just as Valerie was deciding to go to bed there was a loud knock on the front door, followed by three short rings. Valerie flew to the door. There was only one person who would announce his arrival like that, as she remembered from her early days, when Uncle Don was a frequent visitor.

He stood now on the doorstep, tall, bronzed, and looking as excited as any schoolboy home for the holidays.

"Uncle Don!" cried Valerie, and at that moment her mother appeared, with her pretty short curly hair tumbled, and wearing a gay housecoat she had made from re-dyed curtain material.

For the next few minutes all was excitement and confusion, as several suitcases and cardboard boxes were carried indoors by a liveried chauffeur.

"I'm a rogue, turning up at this time of night," Uncle Don said. "Should have been here by tea-time if it hadn't been for the storm. Came through two water splashes, had a burst tyre on our way from the coast, and, well, here I am.

"I suppose you can give me a doss down for the night, eh?" he enquired, when they were seated in the dining-room.

"Of course. What a question!" said Mrs. Barclay, colour in her pale cheeks, as she bustled about making coffee, while Valerie got out the cakes she had made for the twins.

This was a midnight adventure and no mistake!

It turned out to be even more exciting when Uncle Don told them he had been lucky enough to rent a house "Somewhere in Devonshire", close to the sea.

"We'll soon put some colour into those cheeks," he remarked, not in the least deceived by his sister's flushed looks and bright eyes.

Valerie smiled brightly, yet, deep down, she hid a curious sense of disappointment. Of course, Uncle Don's plan was a wonderful one for Mums and the twins; in the ordinary way she would have been as excited as anyone at the prospect of the rest of the summer spent in glorious Devon.

But Diana's tempting invitation put quite a different complexion on the matter. If she went with Mums and the rest, she would miss the holiday of her dreams—a trip by plane and all the unknown joys of visiting a foreign country for the first time.

And then another thought came to the schoolgirl, as she poured out more coffee and handed round cakes. The question of clothes!

Thanks to her own and her mother's skill, her wardrobe was not entirely destitute of pretty frocks. For Devonshire the flowered cottons, gay play-suits, made cunningly from left-overs or made-over from other garments, would be quite in order.

But for a trip to Paris, and in comparison with Diana's smart outfits, oh no!

"I'll have to say 'no' to Diana, anyway," thought Valerie, when at last she was in her own room.

But next morning, in the twinkling of an eye, gloom changed to joy, when after a late breakfast Uncle Don plumped a good-sized suitcase and two deep cardboard boxes at Valerie's feet.

"A few trifles I guess you and your mother can do with," he announced, his eyes twinkling with fun.

A few seconds later Valerie was uttering squeals of joy, as she lifted layers of tissue paper and revealed something which seemed even brighter than the morning sunshine. She lifted the "something" from the case, and was surrounded in folds of pale yellow net, as she unwrapped the ballet-length dress from its wrappings.

Beneath it were undies, nylons, a pair of golden sandals, "fit for a Princess", as Mrs. Barclay remarked when she peeped over Valerie's shoulder.

Two flowery silk frocks apiece, and many other attractive "trifles" as Uncle Don described them, caused more delight. The other suitcase contained presents for Peter and Paul.

"Oh, Uncle Don!" Valerie breathed. Just then the telephone bell shrilled loudly. Still feeling dazed, Valerie ran to answer it.

"Well," came Diana Layton's crisp tones over the wires, "what's the verdict? Say it's yes, or I'm doomed to share a room with a stodgy second cousin of Dad's."

"Well," Valerie began, and then did not know how to go on.

"After Uncle Don's kindness, I just can't refuse to go to Devonshire," she said, when at last she had explained everything to her friend.

"What's all this?" came in Uncle Don's deep, kindly voice from the doorway. "What's this you can't do to Uncle Don?"

Valerie turned from the phone, and after one glance at the cheery, understanding face, she told him of Diana's offer.

"Miss a trip like that?" replied Uncle Don, and his deep chuckle filled the hall. "Devonshire will keep till you come back. Go to it, girl. Tell your chum it's a date," he said, with a pretendedly stern look at Valerie's flushed face.

"And when you've finished we'll go and fetch the lads from the station," he added, as he turned away.

Needless to say, Peter and Paul regarded Uncle Don's timely return as "simply smashing". And when later he decided to settle in Devonshire for good, with Mrs. Layton to keep house for him, there were rejoicings all round.

I-B-G—G

# The Mystery of Titmouse Cottage

### By VIOLET M. METHLEY

IT didn't seem possible, Linnet thought, that she and her mother were having lunch at the little tea-shop near Victoria Station only two hours ago.

Now the omnibus had carried them into country as green as itself: soon they would reach Moonacre.

"And then for Titmouse Cottage!" Linnet sighed happily. "Doesn't it sound silly and funny and cosy, Mother? Just the place we always planned to live in, dropped into our very mouths, just at the right time!"

"Rather a big mouthful!" Mrs. Grant laughed. "But poor Aunt Janet's legacy couldn't have come at a better moment certainly."

"To think I'd scarcely heard of her till the lawyer's letter came and you hadn't seen her for thirty years!"

"No: she never seemed to want us to come down. She'd quarrelled with her brother—my father—of course. But I was wrong not to make another effort——"

"I'm sure you *weren't*!" Linnet shook her brown head decidedly. "Why, her will said: 'because she has never pestered me, I leave to my niece, Rosamond Grant, my cottage at Moonacre, with all its contents in money, furnishings and personal effects, together with the garden and all the birds that dwell therein.'"

"You know it all by heart, dear."

"Because I like it so much, especially the bit about the birds. She *must* have been nice to put that in. . . . Oh, I can just imagine Titmouse Cottage! Whitewash and thatch and old-fashioned furniture, with flowery chintzes and copper warming-pans and——"

"Here we are!" Mrs. Grant interrupted, and Linnet was out and lifting down the suitcases almost before the omnibus drew up in Moonacre village.

She hardly noticed a boy who stood on the path, until he spoke rather shyly.

"I say, are you the Grants?"

"Yes. I'm Linnet and this is my mother," Linnet answered.

"I'm Tony Corbett. My father's the vicar, you know, and old Miss Simson's executor. So I came to show you the way to the cottage. It's quite close, next to the vicarage."

"That's very kind of you," Mrs. Grant said.

"Mr. Collins, the lawyer, has only just left," Tony went on, picking up the two heaviest suitcases. "He and Dad were going through things at the cottage, and Dad's still there."

Walking down the village street, Linnet had time to decide that she liked the look of Tony, with his freckles, rough fair hair and pleasant friendly smile.

"How old are you?" she asked. "I'm not quite fifteen."

"I'm just past. We ought to be—well, friends, don't you think, living so near. Miss Simson rather liked me, although she was a bit queer. . . . Oh, I say, I forgot she was your relation! I'm sorry!"

"We don't mind, do we, Mother? We didn't really know her, you see," Linnet said.

"People here called her a miser." Tony spoke slowly.

"So Mr. Collins wrote to me," Mrs. Grant answered. "He said she never banked any money, but kept it all in the cottage and spent so little that he thought she must have saved quite a lot."

"I hope so," Tony said. "I s'pose your furniture's coming down by road?"

"We haven't any—it was all blitzed," Linnet answered. "We've lived in rooms ever since the war."

"We thought the cottage was furnished, though," Mrs. Grant said.

"Well, in a way. But it's all rather shabby. Miss Simson hated spending money on repairs. Here we are!"

He pushed open a gate. A thatched, whitewashed cottage stared at them through blank uncurtained windows, across an overgrown flower-patch.

"I'm afraid this garden's awfully untidy," Tony apologised. "I've helped with the vegetables at the back—they're pretty good. Miss Simson never bothered about flowers and let the thistles and dandelions run wild, for the birds' sake. Oh, here's Dad!"

The tall, thin grey-haired clergyman came quickly down the path. A sharp-faced, sharp-eyed woman watched the meeting from the porch of a bungalow next door.

"Welcome to Moonacre," the vicar said, his kind face anxious and worried. "I'm afraid—but come in, come in!"

It did not take long to go over the four-roomed cottage, but with every step Linnet's spirits sank lower. Where were the chintzes and old-world furniture she had imagined? Nothing in these rooms, but the barest necessities in the way of beds, chairs and tables; no curtains, scarcely any rugs or carpets. . . .

"But I always heard my aunt had such nice things—pictures, china, silver." Mrs Grant looked round, dismayed.

"She did—years ago," Mr. Corbett said. "But she's sold nearly everything, bit by bit."

"Was she so badly off?"

"No, no! It was just that she disliked many possessions and preferred the money they brought in."

"Well, it's rather a disappointment." Mrs. Grant tried to sound cheerful. "But we must use some of her money to make the place habitable, that's all."

"I'm afraid there's more bad news." The vicar shook his head. "Mr. Collins and I searched the cottage thoroughly, even up chimneys and under floorboards, for the savings we know Miss Simson kept here. But all we found is three shillings and fourpence halfpenny in an old teapot."

Half an hour later Linnet and her mother were alone, having refused the vicarage tea invitation. They had brought a picnic basket and, while the kettle boiled, talked over the future.

"We can just manage for a little while," Mrs. Grant said. "Later, I must find a job—if nothing turns up."

"It ought to be cheap living here, Mother, darling—no rent and plenty of fruit and vegetables. Tony says he'll get rabbits for us, too, and there'll be mushrooms and things. Besides," Linnet added resolutely, "we're going to find that money somehow. Tony's sure it must be somewhere in the house or garden."

"Ho! He is, is he?" A new voice broke in. Their neighbour stood in the open kitchen doorway, staring round inquisitively. "I couldn't help but hear what you said. Mrs. Fenton's my name. I just dropped in to see if I could get tea for you."

"Thanks, but we've just made it. Will you have a cup?" Mrs. Grant said.

"Well, I don't mind if I do." Inside the cottage Mrs. Fenton's eyes were nearly as active as her tongue, as she told them in detail of the accident which had caused Miss Janet Simson's death.

"All because she wouldn't pay a man to do a bit of papering and white-washing! Fell off the ladder, knocked her head, and never really came round again, poor soul! Sad, being all alone like that—but she always kep' to herself—'cause of having all her money in the house, I s'pose. Suspicious of everybody—except the right one, *I* think!"

"You don't know where she kept the money, I suppose?" Linnet burst out impulsively, and Mrs. Fenton tossed her head.

"Me? No! I'm not a Nosey Parker," she declared. "But since you mention it, I'd ask Master Tony, if I was you."

"*He* doesn't know! He's going to help us look."

"Hm!" Mrs. Fenton sniffed. "Always in an' out he's been—working in the garden, too, *and* feeding the birds. All for love—I *don't* think. What he don't know about 'er ways *and* means—well!"

"My aunt loved birds, didn't she?" Mrs. Grant asked.

"Liked 'em better than 'umans, she always said. I never encourage 'em myself—dirty, mucky things, gobbling up all the fruit. Once begin feeding 'em and they're always 'anging round."

"Oh, but we like them, too. We always fed them in London, didn't we, Mother? We'll hang up a bone for the tits and soon they'll be quite tame."

"Tame enough already, if you ask me!" snorted Mrs. Fenton. "In and out the windows, those titmice, pecking at the milk-bottle tops and even letters and newspapers lying on the mats, bold as brass! It was leaving the front-room windows open to the birds and wind that made it in such a mess and not much better for the little she did to it, poor old thing! Well, I must be off—and don't you be too sure Master Tony doesn't know more than he pretends. Some's deep!"

"I don't like her!" Linnet said decidedly after their neighbour's departure. "Did she really want us to think that *Tony* had taken the money?"

"It sounded like it. Jealousy of his being a favourite with Aunt Janet, I daresay."

"P'raps; but she's an old cat, anyway—trying to make mischief like that."

During the next few days, almost the whole village dropped in at Titmouse Cottage, all more or less curious about its money matters. But Linnet's favourite visitors, apart from Tony and his father, were the wonderful birds.

The garden was full of them, their songs and chirpings. Starlings fought over bones and potato-peelings, tits performed acrobatics about a little bag full of fat scraps and bacon-rinds, while finches revelled in the overgrown thistles and sunflowers.

They came indoors, too, as Mrs. Fenton had warned them. Whenever the door of the front room was opened there followed a soft flutter and whirr of wings.

"Much as I love the little darlings, they're rather *too* thoroughly at home in there," Linnet told her mother ruefully. "Do you know, they've pecked at the plaster and paper on the walls, torn off bits here and there, I suppose to get at the limewash or paste. Certainly it's a frightfully ugly cheap paper—perhaps the tits have better taste than poor old Aunt Janet! Anyway, we'll have it off and put the room to rights—directly we've found the money."

" 'When will that be'?" Mrs. Grant quoted sadly.

"I'm sure I don't know." Linnet laughed. "Quite soon, I hope."

But she did not feel quite so confident as she sounded, for the treasure hunt started by Tony and herself had already covered almost every inch of the cottage and garden without the slightest result.

The two had become great friends, for the vicarage, where an elderly aunt kept house for her brother and his motherless son, was a quiet place for a boy's upbringing.

"We've dug over the garden thoroughly and cleared away masses of weeds, searching for the money—so *that's* all to the good!" Linnet leant on her spade after a strenuous afternoon's work. "But it really looks as though Mrs. Fenton's hated enemies, the birds, have flown away with it!"

"Ma Fenton looks at me these days as though I were a loathsome variety of tit or sparrow," Tony grinned. "Which reminds me that some of the other village folk are rather odd in manner. Don't know why, but —— Hullo, Linnet! I believe you've some idea what it means. Yes, you do—your face gives you away. Come on, out with it!"

Red and confused, Linnet tried to laugh it off, but she found herself obliged to confess.

"It's nothing really, only—well, Mrs. Fenton did say something—the day we came——"

"About me? And nasty, too. Tell me!"

Reluctantly Linnet did so.

"I was frightfully angry at the time," she added. "Now I know you, I'd be angrier still."

"Good old Lin! Then *you* don't believe I made up to the poor old lady, just to steal her money?"

"Of course not—it's just Mrs. Fenton's horrid mind and her gossiping ways. But we *must* prove to everybody that you're not a thief and—what can have become of the money?"

"Goodness knows!" Tony shrugged his shoulders. "It's not as if she ever went out and she'd no Post Office account—Father and Mr. Collins made sure of that. But I'm certain it's somewhere and that she meant you to find and have it. She used to say your mother would be surprised to know how much she saved, by spending so little on herself, poor old soul!"

"Dear me! And I do so want to get the cottage nice for Mother!" Linnet sighed. "She's not had a home of her own for so long, but one must have money to do anything really—even make a start."

These plans were much on Linnet's mind and at last she felt she simply couldn't wait any longer. She must make a start—just get one room into order. After all, whitewash and distemper didn't cost much.

"We'll begin on the front room, clean it up, collect the best bits of furniture there——"

"And Dad says we could lend you some bits and pieces from the vicarage—there's an armchair and a small table I could mend up splendidly," Tony broke in on Linnet's confidences. "And Aunt Charlotte thought there were some curtains."

"It *is* good of them," Linnet said gratefully. "Then I'll fix the best time to start."

This, however, settled itself, when Mrs. Grant was summoned, at a few hours' notice, to escort an elderly relative to the seaside and settle her in lodgings. She would be away three or four days.

"Just time, if we work hard, to get the room finished as a surprise for her when she comes back!" Linnet told Tony.

To her surprised disappointment, he flushed red and mumbled uncomfortably.

"Sorry—but I'll be away all tomorrow."

"Oh, Tony, must you? I counted on you."

"I know—but I must go. It's important." Tony looked stubborn.

"And my job isn't, I suppose! Well, I never thought you'd be so mean, Tony. Oh, well, it doesn't matter a bit. I can get on perfectly well without you! Don't bother."

"I won't—I knew you'd be able to manage," Tony retorted—which resulted in something very much like a downright quarrel, for nothing would move him.

He went off whistling in a defiant way, and Linnet decided it just showed you couldn't trust anybody.

Very well. She'd get up at six o'clock tomorrow, work hard and just show him!

Linnet kept to her resolve, although it was something of an effort to roll out of bed at six in the chilly dawn.

After a hurried but heartening breakfast, she carried a pail of warm water into the front room to help in stripping the gaudy patterned paper from the walls.

Her entry was greeted by the usual flutter and flurry of wings. One gay and impertinent tit even remained, perched on the sill, cocking his head at her.

"Yes, Master Impudence!" Linnet shook her fist at him. "But you're not going to fly in and out quite so boldly, once this room is straight. I never saw such a mess as you've made of it!"

She pushed her step-ladder up against the wall and set to work, standing on the top. It oughtn't to take very long, she thought. Poor old Miss Simson had not done the job very well and the tits had undone it only too efficiently.

"The paper doesn't seem to be properly pasted all over—only stuck to the wall in places," Linnet thought. "That's why those little wretches were able to pick bits off so easily with their sharp beaks. I don't believe she stripped all the old paper off either: there's some left underneath. What a mess!"

For some time, Linnet mopped and peeled away diligently with warm water and soft cloths, then suddenly she gave a startled exclamation and almost fell from the high perch.

"Mustn't fall like Aunt Janet!" Linnet thought, staring at the last piece of wall she had exposed.  Under the gaudy flowered paper showed a piece of thin, white paper, covered with black writing.

For a long time Linnet sat motionless, trying to make certain that she really saw what was written there: then with very shaky fingers she began again carefully to peel off the damp wall-paper.

.      .      .      .      .

It was late afternoon and Linnet was still busy, so busy that she never heard a step on the path outside, never knew that anyone was there, until a shadow fell across the patch of sunshine in which she sat, at the foot of the step-ladder.

She gave a little startled cry and clutched in a dazed, half-frightened way at the strips of paper which absolutely surrounded her, on the floor and in her lap.

"Why, what's the matter?  Anyone would think I was a burglar!" Tony's voice said.  "You've not hurt yourself, have you?  You look absolutely daft!"

"I feel so," Linnet said.  "Oh, Tony, I'm so glad you've come!  You can tell me if I'm mad, or if I really see what I think I do.  Look—just look at all this!"

"My goodness!" Tony, too, was staring now.  "Where on earth did you get all that money from?"

"It's—it's Aunt Janet's legacy!"  Linnet spoke with a little gasp.

"*What!*"

"It *is*, Tony; it must be.  She'd fastened them all on to the wall—with sticking-paper, dabs of paste or drawings-pins and then covered them over with that awful wall-paper.  Oh, she must have thought it the cleverest hiding-place—but the tits were cleverer still.  They pecked it away with their sharp little beaks—look! Some of the notes are torn by them."

"Ten-pound notes, fivers, ones and tens!" Tony was checking over the piles. "And you'd never have found them except for the tits!"

"Most likely not—or not until they were destroyed by damp and mould. But I can't understand, Tony—didn't Aunt Janet *want* us to find the money?"

"Of course she did—only, don't you see, she had that fall directly the job was finished, before she'd had time to write any letter or message to Dad or Mr. Collins. I'm sure that's how it was. She wanted to hide the money from possible thieves so that you shouldn't lose it."

"Yes, I expect so," Linnet agreed. "And now, Tony, will you count it. I feel so muddle-headed I can't be sure I was right."

For some time Tony checked and counted diligently. At last he looked up.

"Seven hundred and sixty-eight pounds," he said.

"Then I *was* right," Linnet said in awestruck tones. "But, oh, Tony, I *do* wish you'd been here today to find it with me! It would have been much more fun than doing it alone."

"Wish I had," Tony muttered, reddening. "Because—well—it was just waste of time my going up now you've found all this."

"What do you mean? No, Tony, you've got to tell me! Why did you go to London?"

"To get this." Out of his pocket Tony dragged a packet and thrust it into Linnet's hand. "Oh, don't bother to count: it's twenty-five pounds, just nothing now! But I thought I'd hide it somewhere and let you find it and—and pretend it was the legacy——"

"How *did* you get it?"

"Oh, it's mine honestly enough. I'd a goodish stamp collection—not my own, left me by an uncle, and I sold it. I never wanted the thing a bit."

"Oh, Tony! And I was such a pig to you about today! It's *much* too good of you. But I—we—can't take it."

"If you don't I'll burn it!—not that you want a silly twenty-five pounds now. But I won't take it back."

"Then I know what we'll do—spend it on this room, have it all ready as your present to Mother and me, as a surprise when she comes back," Linnet said decidedly.

"Yes—I'd like that," Tony agreed. "So it's all cleared up." Linnet gave a sigh of relief. "And, oh, Tony, what a lovely end to the mystery of Titmouse Cottage."

———————

# THE AWFUL MISS GRAYSON

## By H. M. CROSS

MARY PERRY glanced at her watch. Looking at Aunt Dot across the dinner table she began, "This time tomorrow——" Aunt Dot laughed.

"I know—the school choir will be trembling in its shoes. You've said it so often this week that I know it by heart!"

Mary chuckled and made a wry face. "Poor Aunt Dot, you'll be as relieved as I when the competition is over."

Her aunt smiled and nodded. She knew how keen Mary was to win a coveted place in the team of twelve singers to be selected tomorrow from the school choir by a visiting judge. The successful candidates would appear in an annual charity concert held at Rathwood, a nearby town, along with other teams from the various school choirs.

This year the concert had assumed greater importance than ever, for it was to be broadcast. Mary, who was living with her aunt while her parents were abroad had a very special reason for wanting to be in the team. The broadcast fell on the very day of her mother's birthday. It would be wonderful to feel that Mummy was actually hearing her voice over the air.

Half an hour later, as Mary struggled out of her Wellingtons at school, Jennifer Bond dashed into the cloakroom. Mary knew at once by the expression on her friend's face that she had some important news.

"Guess who is judging us tomorrow!" Jennifer burst out, and then, not waiting—"that awful Miss Grayson." She shuddered. "I've got stage fright already; the idea of singing before Miss Grayson gives me the jim-jams—you know how eccentric she is."

Mary nodded seriously as her friend paused for breath. Miss Grayson, a a brilliant musician, founder of the Rathwood Choral Society, was well known for her peculiar ways. Then Mary smiled.

"Oh, Miss Grayson can't be too bad or she wouldn't keep any members in the Society and, anyway, she should be an excellent judge of singing."

"I suppose you are right," answered Jennifer somewhat gloomily, "but that doesn't comfort me. One look from Miss Grayson and I'm sure my voice will die of fright!"

The choir girls were already assembled in the music room when the two friends entered. Then, as Miss Brown their choir mistress and music teacher bustled in, the hum of conversation ceased.

"You all know this is the final practice," said Miss Brown crisply after the girls had hurried to their allotted positions. "We will rehearse the competition piece first, taking the solos afterwards in the order already set down in the judges' list."

Miss Brown sat down at the piano and played the familiar opening bars. After weeks of practice the choir confidently took their cue.

"It's perfect," thought Mary, as their voices rang out in perfect harmony. She felt a glow of pride as the tricky bar in the middle was negotiated without difficulty. As the music reached its climax, however, neither she nor anyone else noticed a figure in a dripping mackintosh slip in by the rear door.

And no one noticed the visitor silently depart as the final notes of the last soloist died away. Miss Brown, beaming with pride and satisfaction, complimented her choir on a really splendid performance.

"If we do as well tomorrow, the judge will have a difficult job in selecting," Mary told herself thoughtfully after she had waved to Jennifer and was hurrying along the wet deserted road. She was a little later than usual and it was already getting dusk; Aunt Dot would be anxious. Besides, she was eager to tell her aunt how well the rehearsal had gone. Suddenly she decided to take the short cut across the fields.

At length, nearing the stile which led into the road near her home, a whine of distress made Mary stop. It seemed to come from the far corner of the field. Yes, there it was again. A plaintive, whine accompanied by a splashing sound which made her heart leap, for it came from the direction of the pond. Thick with mud and water-weeds, Mary knew how treacherous it was with its deceptive, sloping banks.

In a trice she had turned and was running across the marshy ground. Reaching the dark-looking stretch of water she could just discern a small, muddy dog lying exhausted on a little island of twigs quite near the edge.

"You poor little thing," cried Mary, darting forward. The dog wagged its tail feebly. Then as Mary stretched to lift him her foot slipped on the treacherous mud; she stumbled and almost fell headlong into the slimy water. Miraculously she regained her balance and caught hold of the dog's collar, but not before a deluge of muddy water half drenched her.

"It's lucky you are small," Mary told the bedraggled animal shivering in her arms. He licked her nose with a tiny pink tongue and whined.

As Mary made her way back across the field she examined the animal's collar. In the fading light she could just make out the words "THE ELMS, LITTLE MEAD". Mary uttered an exclamation of surprise, for The Elms,

a large, isolated house on the outskirts of the village, was occupied by Miss Grayson.

She thought of Miss Grayson anxiously searching and at a brisk pace she set off towards The Elms. The dog yelped excitedly as Mary approached the massive front door some twenty minutes later—he knew he was home. Before Mary had time to push the old-fashioned bell the door opened and a little silver-haired woman appeared. The dog wriggled frantically, and with a joyous bark leapt from Mary's arms and hurled himself forward.

As the little woman stooped to pick him up with a smile of relief it was obvious to Mary that he had found his mistress. So this was the awful Miss Grayson!

"I've been so worried," Miss Grayson smilingly confided to Mary. "Do come in and tell me how you found him, I'm really most grateful."

"Thank you, I mustn't stay, Aunt will be getting awfully worried, she doesn't know where I am," replied Mary hurriedly. "So, if you will excuse me, I think I ought to be going."

"Well, good-bye, and thank you very much indeed," said Miss Grayson warmly.

.    .    .    .    .    .

"It's funny," remarked Aunt Dot as she later listened to Mary while she helped her out of her wet clothes. "Somehow I didn't think Miss Grayson the kind of person to have pets."

"I think it's a good sign, anyhow," declared her niece. "I don't think she is such an ogre after all."

Mary awoke next morning with a feeling that something was not quite right. She felt hot and shivery in turns. Her throat hurt her and her head ached. The worst had happened! "Today!" she moaned miserably. "To have a cold today of all days!"

Aunt Dot's firm verdict was "Bed!"

Mary felt too wretched to object. Tears of disappointment trickled down her nose.

"Never mind," her aunt consoled her gently. "It can't be helped. You can try for the concert next year."

"Oh, it wouldn't be the same as this time, Auntie, with Mummy's favourite piece, and broadcast on her birthday!"

She felt very very depressed. Nevertheless, after a hot drink of her aunt's delicious concoction of blackcurrant and honey she did manage to drop into a troubled doze. She awoke to the sound of familiar footsteps pelting up the stairs. The next minute Jennifer burst into the bedroom with scant respect for the invalid.

"Just take a look at this," she cried gaily, waving a paper at Mary. "Guaranteed to cure all fits of the blues!"

"Whatever are you on about?" Mary stifled a sneeze and managed a croaky laugh. She felt better already; Jennifer's nonsense was as good as a tonic.

"You'll never guess what has happened," Jennifer ran on as she plumped on the bed. "Miss Grayson did one of her eccentric acts yesterday. She thought we should all sing better if we didn't realise we were being judged, so she sneaked in during the rehearsal and heard everything!"

Jennifer paused for breath and grinned at Mary's astonished exclamation. "It's true. Miss Brown told us this morning. And here's the list of the winners—read it."

Jennifer gurgled delightedly as Mary read the list incredulously.

Sure enough her own name was there.

"Isn't it marvellous?" crowed Jennifer. "We're both in the team. But that isn't all—guess what?" Mary shook her head helplessly. Things were a little too much for her.

"You've been chosen to sing the solo!" and she flourished another paper at her friend's dumbfounded face.

Mary's eyes misted with tears. It seemed too wonderful to be true.

And that was what Mrs. Perry herself thought as she switched her radio on a month later and her daughter's voice—trained to perfection by a grateful Miss Grayson—came clearly over the air. A wonderful birthday present!

I-B-G—H

# A DEARTH of GIRLS

## By Marjorie P. Whitaker

THE door of the Seniors' study was flung open and Cherry Vince flounced in.

"You know I sometimes think it would be so peaceful if I could have this study to myself," expostulated Eugene Beardsley, looking up from her French prose.

"Sorry, I didn't know you were here! You'd be fearfully dull, and there'd be no one to stop your writing verse when you ought to be working. Anyhow, as school captain, you're bound to share with me whilst I'm games captain." Cherry grinned, her hazel eyes dancing. Then, becoming serious, she flung herself into the cane chair and frowned.

Eugene retrieved a grip in her brown hair and glanced across at her chum. "Something's wrong—what is it?" Eugene's eyes twinkled.

"The Easter term is sent to try us. It always makes life difficult. People crock themselves up in the previous term and get exhausted in

this, and some people don't come back after the holidays because of in-
fection that they've contracted, or they're in quarantine. In this term
there's always a dearth of new girls, as you know, so my brain is just about
cracked, wondering what's going to happen," Cherry ended breathlessly.

"The fate of Millard Abbey always hangs heavily on the games
captain in the Easter term, I admit. But wait and see what turns up
when the new lot come in. I expect they're unpacking with Matron,"
Eugene said consolingly.

Cherry retied her shoe-laces. "But it's the worst of all possible bad
luck that Marcia Hetherington had to fall off her bike the very day before
we were due back at school. Some people ought to be led about by a
nurse during the holidays. She won't be any use until the summer term
and then she'll probably have to have a runner; and she'll be no good at
tennis—she never is!"

"My goodness! Aren't you a pessimist! Can't you think of one bright
spot anywhere? I've never known you so miserable as this before!"

"But things couldn't be worse. Unless one of the new lot turns out to
be as good as Marcia or Barbara Peel, or Cath or Nessie! Oh! what's the
use! Barbara's gone abroad; we'll never have a lacrosse right wing as
good as Babs. And Cath's such a splendid reliable sort, and Nessie's so
quick—no wonder we did so well in all our matches before. But the
future will be sheer disgrace for Millard Abbey, you see!" groaned Cherry.

"What's going on? May we come in?" someone called.

"Don't sit on that, it's fragile! It has a loose leg. There now! Why
don't you wait until you're invited to sit down?" laughed Eugene as
Fiona Dewar, a plump rosy-cheeked girl, fell with a thud on the floor.

"Get up. I'll fix it. You want a nail in it. Why have a stool taking
up room if it's not fit to sit on!" Janet Fearnless said, helping Fiona to
her feet.

"Yes, and have every visitor sitting on nails and then complain of
torn tunics. We had that last term. If you will only sit on the stool
carefully and keep still, nothing will happen, but when people barge in

and bound on to it, especially if they're heavyweights, it serves them right if it gives way," Cherry said, grinning.

"Don't take any notice of her; she's in a black mood," Eugene remarked.

"I'm not too heavy for my height; at least, not much," Fiona protested in an offended tone, adding, addressing Cherry: "Why should you be so grumpy first day of term?"

Cherry leaned back in her chair, stretching out her slim legs. "Oh, tell the infant, somebody—you, Eugene—all about my little troubles, and perhaps Fiona with her little wand can waft them all away."

"Tell her yourself. Might do you good to keep talking. Might relieve your feelings," Eugene returned placidly.

Footsteps and voices in the corridor caused each girl to look towards the door expectantly, and in a moment Bertha Drew, a prefect, appeared along with two other girls.

"I've brought Myrtle and Violet Needham. They're twins. They are going in Five A."

There was an involuntary exclamation from Cherry, partially stifled, because the twins were so remarkably unlike each other. Violet was a pretty fair-haired girl with delicately formed features, whilst the other girl had dark hair and a sturdy russet complexion. She would have appeared attractive but for her mutinous mouth. But what struck the others was the obvious difference in temperament.

Violet was completely at ease, ready to chatter, whilst Myrtle was silent, almost truculent.

"Well, I hope you'll be able to help us. Here's Cherry Vince, our games captain. She'd like to ask you about games," Eugene said kindly.

"Well, we'll leave you to it. I don't think there are any more to come among the Seniors," Bertha said, as Janet and Fiona stood up.

"We're both awfully keen on games, so you can put us down for everything," Violet suggested with a charming smile.

"You'll be tried out for everything in due course. Let's hope you'll be valuable for at least one game," Cherry returned imperturbably.

Eugene turned to the bookshelves to hide her amusement. Cherry was never impressed by anyone's assertion of keenness until she had seen them play. After asking what position Violet had played in for winter and summer games, it was apparent that Violet was making all the answers for herself and also for her twin. Cherry threw a comical, helpless glance at Eugene, who came to the rescue with: "How many girls were there at your last school, Myrtle?"

"Oh, hoards! I hate a crowd. There were about five hundred!" Violet broke in.

"Just a moment, please. I'm speaking to Myrtle," Eugene replied with dignity.

An inscrutable expression flitted across Myrtle's face as she replied flatly: "We've been to eleven schools and had five governesses."

"Don't be stupid, Myrtle!" her twin began hastily, with an appealing glance.

"Ah! Does that mean you're merely here to give Millard Abbey a short trial? In that case, I don't think we need to go on delving into your games history. It's hardly worth Miss Hailey, our games mistress, working and coaching you, if you're going to leave us soon," Cherry said in disappointment, scarcely able to conceal her disgust.

"Oh, but we always mean to stay, but we get tired of a school so quickly, but we're always hoping that we'll find the right one. I'm sure this must be it!" gushed Violet.

"There's the bell for tea. You've a long way through the corridors—better hurry," Eugene urged, hoping to stave off Cherry's explosive comments that she knew were due.

Were the situation not so serious, Eugene would have been amused at the droll expression on Cherry's piquant face.

"I know all you're feeling. Spare me everything. But I'd like to say this. If we can break down Myrtle's reserve I think we're going to like her better than her twin. Myrtle's trouble is that she is overshadowed by sweet Violet. She ought to assert herself."

Cherry kicked the unoffending stool, and then, arm in arm, the captains flung themselves off for what they deemed a good tea as some slight consolation.

The following day there was a trial lacrosse match made up of a scratch crowd, which included the twins, who played quite a creditable game, but Myrtle was obviously the better of the two.

Soon after the whistle blew, Violet was over-anxiously determined to put up a brilliant show, and when Janet snatched the ball and sent a long shot towards goal, she bit her lip with vexation as the goal-keeper failed to stop it. "Oh dear! I'm so sorry! I ought not to have let Janet get it from me," she wailed.

After that she seemed to fall to pieces. "If anything goes wrong in the first half, it worries me dreadfully," she said to no one in particular.

But Myrtle, on the right wing, put up a plucky fight for the opposing team, and she played with quick judgment. She streaked up and down the field until she had the ball safely, and in a few moments there was a yell of "Goal!" as with a skilful shot she sent the ball skimming up the field and scored.

Afterwards the girls discussed the efforts of the twins. "We can't judge on one game, but, up to a point, Violet is all right. The trouble is, she won't, in my opinion, be dependable. She seemed ready to burst into tears at half-time," Cherry said.

After a couple of weeks, during which time there were several practice matches, it was decided to play Myrtle in the fixture against Alden College. To Cherry's astonishment, after the list was put up, Myrtle burst into the study, evidently moved from her habitual calm, which almost bordered on sulkiness.

"Please, I shan't be able to play in that match. I have my private reasons ; and, anyhow, there are enough without me. I mean you can choose someone else—Violet, for instance, plays a very good game sometimes."

Cherry glared unbelievingly at the girl, who was obviously embarrassed under Cherry's scrutiny.

"Do you realise that a Fifth Former can't just barge in this study without knocking and then offer advice which hasn't been asked for? You're down to play because of your usefulness and you're my choice. Now cut along and leave me in peace before Eugene comes back to strangle her violin. What I have to put up with, no one knows!" Cherry ended good humouredly.

Myrtle's mouth took on stubborn lines. "If I can't play, whom will you choose? Please choose Violet. She can play awfully well, really."

"Violet's not in the running. Unless there's a mighty catastrophe, you will play in all matches this term—because we've no one up to your standard. You needn't get swell-headed about that; it's the sad fact that one of our best girls, who is even better than you, is away this term. So it's up to you, Myrtle. You must play your best for Millard Abbey."

Without another word, Myrtle strode away, leaving Cherry perplexed and suspicious. "I believe Violet is at the bottom of this," she murmured.

That night in number five dormitory, Janet, who slept in the end cubicle near the door, was awakened by an unusual noise.

At first she thought she was mistaken, for, as she told herself, "Myrtle is too reserved to howl like a junior, but just then she heard Myrtle toss, making her bed creak.

Janet peeped through the curtains and whispered: "Are you all right? Anything—er—wrong?"

For reply there was a sniff and a gulp.

"Myrtle, may I come in?" Janet asked, taking permission for granted. After all, as prefect she had the right to investigate.

"Oh, please leave me alone," Myrtle whispered, choking back a sob.

"I must know why you're crying. Do tell me. Quickly, do tell me. I might be able to help you." Janet bent over the girl, who was fighting her tears, dabbing her eyes with a damp ball of a handkerchief.

Gradually the story came out.

"So she wants to leave and go back home to have lessons with a governess again. She's fed up with team games, she says. In future we'll only play tennis, winter and summer. But, you see, I'd so set my mind on staying here and trying for matric. this summer, and I'd even got the idea of hoping for a university scholarship. I want to do economics, but Vi's not keen on one or two of the mistresses. She's already been in trouble over her maths."

"But I don't quite understand. Why do you have to do what Violet wants every time? You say it's always she who wants to change—I think she's a perfect dog in the manger!"

"Well, she has the choice, you see. She's quite sweet, really, but she has to have her own way because she used to be delicate."

"Selfish, I should call her. But surely your parents won't give in this time, when you want to stay so much? It's your turn to have your own way," Janet protested.

"But our parents are in the Far East and won't be home for three years; by that time it will be too late!" Myrtle's eyes filled again.

"You can write or cable or do something, can't you?" Janet demanded exasperatedly.

"No. We are under the charge of a guardian and she says I ought to give in to Violet, as, of course, if her twin had lived, I wouldn't have been adopted and so——"

Janet's eyes popped. "Adopted? Aren't you twins?"

"No, not even unidentical ones. We're cousins exactly the same age. I was adopted when I was six months old, so, you see, I'm indebted to them awfully. If only Vi would stick it here," Myrtle said wistfully.

"Look here, we'll have to go to sleep now. We'll waken the others if we keep on jabbering. Tomorrow I'll have thought of a solution, but we'll have to take Cherry and Eugene into our confidence."

"Oh, but you mustn't do anything to upset Violet."

"Only *you* must be upset, eh? And how do you think you're going to do well in work and games if you spend half the night crying your eyes out?"

The next day, Janet asked Eugene and Cherry to help Myrtle. So it was between tea and prep., when Violet was in the library, that Janet asked her to go along with her to the captain's study.

"I think I know why they want me. I offered to practise long shots with Cherry if she'll only give me another trial for the lacrosse match."

Janet gazed at the pretty face curiously. "Did you honestly? What did Cherry say?"

"As a matter of fact she was rather rude. I don't mind telling you that I think you would make a better games captain than her. However she found herself in that position I don't know. I also don't mind telling you that if we leave here the blame will be put on Cherry Vince. She seems to have gone out of her way to be nasty almost ever since I first saw her."

Janet burst out laughing, to Violet's indignation.

"What are you laughing at?"

"You! You're so funny. There's no knowing what you'll say next. You've got a terrific sense of your

own importance, and mine, too, if you think I could be in Cherry's place."

"But every girl should put a value on herself, otherwise one only gets squashed in a school like this."

"That can happen anywhere. You don't ever try to squash your sister, for instance?" Janet said meaningly.

"Don't be absurd. I'm awfully fond of Myrtle, but she always looks on me as leader, of course."

"Why should she?" Janet asked bluntly.

Violet's blue eyes opened wide. "Well, it always has been so and it always will. One can't change, can one?"

"Yes. Myrtle's changed since she came here, and from what I know of Cherry and Eugene, you'll be changed before you're much older," Janet said wickedly.

"If there's any bullying——" Violet began.

"You want to be the one to do it," Janet interrupted.

"Don't be absurd!"

"Well, here we are, and take my advice and listen carefully to what they have to say, or you'll be up against Dr. Dangerfield, the headmistress," and with that, Janet gently pushed Violet inside the study.

"Goodness! Three prefects, two captains. Having a meeting?" Violet drawled with sarcastic politeness.

Eugene replied earnestly: "We want to deal with you here, rather than let matters go to Dr. Dangerfield. Perhaps that's been the trouble at your other schools. You were expelled from more than one for rebelling against rules and—er—bullying. We think we might be able to put things right for you here before you've had much time to go far wrong, though according to your form reports you've not made a good start, have you?"

The look of astonishment on Violet's face changed to indignation, then to a somewhat shamefaced expression mingled with guilt.

"If you're starting already on me, then this is the worst school I've been to yet," she blurted miserably, her pretty colour coming and going.

"It's better to try and put you right as soon as we can. You can't go on having black marks. You'll be miserable if you don't get a grip on yourself. You've come here to work, not just for yourself, but for the school, and this is where Myrtle comes in. She has ambitions, thank goodness!"

"D'you mind if I butt in? I'd just like to say that it wasn't my fault! I was given marks, but I have ambitions, too. The trouble with me is I've been so unlucky at the schools I've been in. I've never had a chance. In the games here, for instance——"

"This is where I come in!" Cherry said quietly. "Listen! Has anyone ever told you that there is such a thing as 'match temperament'? Because, though you can play lacrosse and hockey, you can't control your feelings. Myrtle can! Copy her and you'll soon be picked for matches. You can't have a better model than Myrtle."

"But——" Violet interposed.

"But we don't want to waste our time with you if you're bent on going on in your old way. Are you willing to try to forget Violet Needham and give a thought to other people? So far our collected reports about you are—domineering, vain, selfish——"

"Oh, stop it! No one's ever said such beastly things to me in all my life!" Violet begged, covering her face with her hands.

In gentle tones, Eugene said: "You've never given anyone the chance to like you in your other schools, that's why."

Violet lifted her puzzled, tear-stained face. "Like me?" she repeated.

"Yes, there is something about you that we like, so we're giving you a chance to make good here. If we had no hope of bringing you up to scratch, we'd ask Dr. Dangerfield to deal with you. We believe you're worth a bit of trouble."

"Oh, Eugene, I think I'll try, but I hardly know how to be any different. Myrtle always gets on with people easily; I don't," Violet replied humbly.

"You won't find us difficult now we've cleared the air before you've had the chance to carry on in your spoiled fashion. I must be straight—it's the only way. Now I want to tell you this. Every girl here is responsible to her House and I want you to give Myrtle a free hand to make what she can of her effort to get on. Will you give us your promise to try to settle down here and in return we'll be ready to help you in any way."

Violet hesitated. "Surely Myrtle hasn't complained about me? I've never known her to do such a thing. She's too sweet natured. But, has she?"

"No," Janet said hurriedly. "But we're not dumb. You must be fair to Myrtle. You must give her a chance to live her own life instead of mismanaging it for her."

"Dear me! I never expected all this sort of thing when I asked my guardian to send us here," Violet said slowly, then with a rush, she continued: "Anyhow, I'll show you what I can do about it. I'm not entirely to blame. I didn't ask people to spoil me."

Cherry broke the tension by laughing. "Well, maybe Myrtle has been too slack and partly to blame for allowing you to sit on her."

Everyone smiled, including Violet. "I think I shall make a go of it here and stick it out." Her eyes twinkled roguishly. "Actually, I intended to, because I've a feeling I might like you in spite of this meeting."

"Because of it, you mean!" Eugene replied sagely.

Violet smiled winningly. "I suppose I ought to thank you for taking me in hand—holding a special meeting about me is rather flattering."

"Not at all," Cherry replied. "There you go again, getting all conceited. Have you forgotten there's a dearth of good all-round girls this term? So we must cultivate the few we've got—which includes you!"

Violet joined in the laughter. "I must find Myrtle," she said, affection in her voice.

"She'll do all right," Eugene said confidently as the door closed.